ACPL, Laramie, W
3909209583710
Harlow, Joan Hia
Breaker boy /
Pieces:1

D0392366

Breaker Boy

Also by Joan Hiatt Harlow

Star in the Storm
Joshua's Song
Shadow on the Sea
Thunder from the Sea
Midnight Rider
Blown Away!
Secret of the Night Ponies
Firestorm!
The Watcher

Breaker Boy

Albany County
Public Library
Laramie, Wyoming

Joan Hiatt Harlow

Margaret K. McElderry Books
New York   London   Toronto   Sydney   New Delhi

MARGARET K. McELDERRY BOOKS
An imprint of Simon & Schuster Children's Publishing Division
1230 Avenue of the Americas, New York, New York 10020

This book is a work of fiction. Any references to historical events, real people, or real places are used fictitiously. Other names, characters, places, and events are products of the author's imagination, and any resemblance to actual events or places or persons, living or dead, is entirely coincidental.

Text copyright © 2017 by Joan Hiatt Harlow
Jacket illustration copyright © 2017 by Jim Madsen

All rights reserved, including the right of reproduction in whole or in part in any form.
MARGARET K. McELDERRY BOOKS is a trademark of Simon & Schuster, Inc.

For information about special discounts for bulk purchases, please contact Simon & Schuster Special Sales at 1-866-506-1949 or business@simonandschuster.com.

The Simon & Schuster Speakers Bureau can bring authors to your live event. For more information or to book an event, contact the Simon & Schuster Speakers Bureau at 1-866-248-3049 or visit our website at www.simonspeakers.com.

Book design by Sonia Chaghatzbanian and Irene Metaxatos
The text for this book was set in Minion Pro.
Manufactured in the United States of America
0917 FFG
First Edition
10 9 8 7 6 5 4 3 2 1
Library of Congress Cataloging-in-Publication Data
Names: Harlow, Joan Hiatt, author.
Title: Breaker boy / Joan Hiatt Harlow.
Description: First edition. | New York : Margaret K. McElderry Books, [2017] | Summary: In 1911 Pennsylvania, Corey, eleven, works in coal mines to help support his family, but when an accident triggers a phobia, he must turn to a strange recluse for help.
Identifiers: LCCN 2016056190
ISBN 9781481465373 (hardback) | ISBN 9781481465397 (eBook)
Subjects: | CYAC: Coal mines and mining—Fiction. | Family life—Pennsylvania—Fiction. | Physicians—Fiction. | Phobias—Fiction. | Rescues—Fiction. | Polish Americans—Fiction. | Pennsylvania—History—20th century—Fiction. | BISAC: JUVENILE FICTION / Historical / United States / 20th Century. | JUVENILE FICTION / Action & Adventure / General. | JUVENILE FICTION / Action & Adventure / Survival Stories.
Classification: LCC PZ7.H22666 Bre 2017 | DDC [Fic]—dc23
LC record available at https://lccn.loc.gov/2016056190

For Claire and Larry Krane . . .
and Django

Contents

Breaker Boy

1
Drowning!

Corey sat on a rock, pulled off his boots, and pushed his feet into the old pair of skates. He looked at the shining surface of the ice and grinned. He had been watching day after day, until the fragile shell of ice on the top hardened as smooth as a mirror. Once the kids who didn't work in the mines realized the ice was safe, they would crowd every puddle and pond around Wilkes-Barre each afternoon and weekend, to play hockey. But for now, Corey had the whole pond to himself—except for a dog somewhere nearby, who kept barking.

After lacing up the skates, he stepped onto the ice, gliding awkwardly around the perimeter of the pond, his ankles folding inward. It was always like this the first time out. Besides, the skates were too tight. His feet had grown a couple of sizes since last winter.

However, he probably wouldn't have much time to skate once he started to work. Corey was eleven—almost twelve—and the oldest boy in the family. Dad tried to put off the inevitable, hoping his sons would never work in the mines. However, Dad told him just a few days ago that the family needed money. There was no way to get around it. Corey would find a job in the mine, and quit school in February, when he turned twelve.

Still, once I start working, maybe I could put something aside for new skates. Maybe a nickel or dime now and then. I'll hide them in the cigar box Dad gave me. "To keep your treasures—your special things," Dad said. *What special things?* Corey remembered opening it, expecting something special inside. It was empty. It remained empty except for a rabbit's foot that he found on the way home from school one rainy day that still stank from the wet fur.

Corey did a quick turn and skated forward again. He stroked across the smooth ice, heading out to the middle of the pond. A few white clouds moved rapidly across the blue sky. He could see the gables of the big house on the hillside, belonging to that strange Mrs. Chudzik, the Polish widow of Dr. Chudzik. Corey heard the kids at school whisper that she was "peculiar." Corey was curious how they knew, since he had never met her. He'd seen her a few times driving around in her bright red touring car with her scary-looking dog at her side, when she went out for groceries or something.

In fact, he had just seen her this morning down by the

company store. A few women standing nearby whispered that the dog in the front seat was Mrs. Chudzik's hellhound. His grandpa told creepy tales about the hellhounds of Wales, where he was born—stories of dogs with blazing eyes and bloody fangs. Poppa, his Polish grandfather, said that if a hellhound looked at you three times, you would probably die in a terrible accident or something worse.

As Corey stood on tiptoes to see the driver of the snappy red convertible, the dog had stared at Corey and bared his teeth. Three times this happened! Corey felt a shiver run down his back at the memory. It was no wonder that everyone in town stayed away from Mrs. Chudzik. Just having the dog bare his teeth was enough to scare the pants off anyone.

No one saw Mrs. Chudzik or her dog very often. Most of the time, she and her dog stayed inside the gloomy gray mansion. But it was also said she had a beak instead of a nose—and when she lured children into her house, they were never heard from again.

Corey turned to do a little circle, when suddenly his blade hit—what? He heard an echoing sound, and he realized, too late, that the ice had cracked and he was falling into a black hole of icy water.

He grabbed for the edge of the opening, and more ice cracked and broke off. He tried to swim, but the waterlogged sleeves of his jacket pulled him deeper into the blackness.

As he sank, he groped for the edge of the hole again, but this time he couldn't find it. The sun shone through the ice above him and everything was bright and blurry. Where was the hole he had fallen through?

His bulky clothes and skates dragged him deeper. He tried to kick his way to the surface, but he could not lift his legs. His pants were full of water and tugging at him; his arms were heavy and tired.

Clouds must have covered the sun, as now it was as dark as a grave. He pressed his mouth near the ice and found a small place of air just under the surface. He must stay close to the top and breathe in that tiny space of air until someone came.

But who would come? No one was around.

It was hard to stay near the pocket of air, with his soaked clothes pulling him under. Terror crept over him, and he panicked. Thrashing, he fought to break the ice above him. His arms and legs were useless and weary, and he found himself slipping, slipping down into the murkiness.

He needed air—he *had to breathe.* He tried to take a breath, but water flooded into his mouth and down into his lungs.

As he nodded out of consciousness, he could hear the barking dog, but when he felt his feet touch the bottom of the pond, he knew he had drowned.

2

The Open Coffin

Corey stirred, took a deep breath, and flailed around, still fighting to break through the ice. He wasn't cold anymore. He was warm and his feet were tangled in a blanket or something.

Had he drowned? Yes. He remembered drowning. So he must be dead!

Where was he? He closed his eyes, trying to remember. He recollected a dog in a red car. He could still see the beast snarling with those sharp teeth—just like the hellhound stories he'd heard. The hellhound had looked at Corey three times this morning. It was true. Corey had gone under the ice and now he was probably dead, just as the stories say.

Had he drowned and gone to heaven? He opened

his eyes. The room he was lying in sure didn't look like how he'd pictured heaven. This place was dark and gloomy.

Maybe there had already been a funeral. He envisioned Mom and Dad wringing their hands and crying. Dad would have to send Corey's younger brothers, Jack and Sammy, to be breaker boys in the mine. Poor Sammy was only six.

Corey shook his head, trying to figure out what had taken place.

I remember falling through the ice and trying to find air. . . . I could hear a dog barking . . . then my skates hit the bottom of the pond. And that's all. So I must be dead.

He sat up on his elbows and looked around. He was in a strange room filled with dark wooden furniture and old paintings of landscapes and people he didn't know. Perhaps this was a funeral parlor. He pushed aside the down quilt that covered him. He had on only his underwear, and that was still damp and clung to his skin. His clothes were gone. His feet had socks—huge dry socks that didn't belong to him. *This can't be a funeral parlor—they dress you up in nice clothes for your own funeral.*

Corey climbed out of the bed. Maybe he could sneak out of this house and find his way home. But he wasn't walking all the way home in his underwear! He looked through the window and saw that it was night. The faint glow of a streetlight flickered in the distance.

He listened for sounds around the house—any sound. Running water? Footsteps? Everything was silent, except for a clock ticking. He opened the door of his room quietly, hardly daring to breathe. A poorly lit hallway stretched out in front of him, and at the end, he could see a carved wooden door, probably to the outside.

Gathering the quilt around him, he crept silently down the hall. *Ticktock. Ticktock.* The deep strokes of a clock ticked in the next room.

As he approached the parlor, he stopped. Was someone in there waiting? He shivered and his teeth chattered and clicked like his grandfather's dentures. Taking a deep breath, he peeked into the big room and froze. In the center of the room was a coffin!

This is a funeral home! But who is in the coffin? Could it be . . . me? Corey stepped into the room, tiptoed across the thick carpet to the coffin, and peered inside.

An elderly woman lay within the polished wooden casket, her body resting on a luxurious pink satin pillow and adornments. Her gray hair, fluffed into curls, accentuated the deep wrinkles that lined her pale face.

Corey stood frozen. Who was she? Then he realized the quilt had fallen onto the floor, and he stood by the coffin in his underwear. What if there were mourners somewhere seated in the dozen or so chairs that stood around the coffin? Grabbing the quilt, he wrapped it around himself.

There was no one there.

Hearing a rustling from the casket, he turned toward the corpse. The dead woman was sitting up, her eyes staring straight at him!

Backing up in horror, Corey screamed, dropped the quilt, and raced for the front door.

3
Mrs. Chudzik

With his fingers fumbling, Corey tried to open the oak door. His sweaty hands shook so badly he couldn't get a grip on the doorknob. Then he realized it was locked.

"Stop right where you are!"

Corey peeked over his shoulder. Standing in the archway to the parlor was the coffin lady, looking very much alive. Her right hand held on to the collar of a large black dog, who strained to lunge at Corey.

"Turn around!" Her deep voice echoed under the high ceilings and bounded off the walls.

Corey turned around with knocking knees. "Yes, ma'am," he sputtered.

"Who are you?"

"Corey . . . Adamski," he stammered. "Where am I?"

"You are in my house," Coffin Lady answered. "Where did you think you were?"

Corey couldn't concentrate on the lady's questions with her dog pulling and moving closer by the minute. "Last thing I remember, I was drowning." He shuddered as the dog showed his teeth.

"Yes, you were drowning, and lucky for you my dog saw you go under and came barking to me. Otherwise you'd be hammering at the golden gates right now." She motioned to him to come back into the parlor. "Sit down," she commanded. As she took a seat, her dog sat by her side. "I wasn't sure you'd make it. I did artificial respiration on you. Darn near broke my back trying to get you to breathe."

"I do remember hearing a dog barking," he said. After a moment, he added, "Thank you . . . for saving me."

"Thank my dog. If he hadn't spotted you, you'd be dead. Now, what are you going to do?"

"I'd like to go home. My folks must be worried." He looked down at his underwear. "Where are my clothes?"

"Drying on the radiators. I couldn't let you stay in those wet clothes, now, could I?"

"Um. No. We don't have a phone, but perhaps you could call someone to get word to my folks."

"I don't have a phone," Coffin Lady interrupted. "Never wanted one. Always ringing. When my husband, the doctor, was alive, that phone never stopped. When he died, I pulled the wires right out of the wall myself. I haven't had a phone since he passed on . . . almost ten years ago."

Now Corey knew he was in the big house with the tur-rets and gables. And the coffin lady was the scary Mrs. Chudzik. He would never have recognized her from seeing her in the car. At that time, she wore a black hooded cape and the tip of her nose was all that was visible.

Corey couldn't move a finger or a toe and his legs were like straws. Standing before him was the very woman he heard caught kids like him . . . and they disappeared for-ever. As he stared at her, unable to speak, he could see her birdlike beak—the one that she used to tear flesh. Her eyes were as black and deadly as the deep water in the pond.

Mrs. Chudzik had spoken, but Corey never heard a word. And he couldn't utter a word either. He just stood there, bewitched.

"Didn't you hear what I asked? Did the water plug up your ears?" she yelled, startling her dog, who snarled and struggled to get to Corey again.

Corey almost slid off his chair. "No—yes. My ears are plugged up from the water," he lied. "Excuse me? What—did you ask me?"

Enunciating each syllable and with a loud voice, she said, "Do you want me to take you home? It's dark outside."

"Yes, yes, please take me home," Corey begged. "I'm supposed to be home when the streetlights go on."

Mrs. Chudzik motioned him back down the hall to the bedroom where he had been. She turned on the light, grabbed his clothes off a radiator, and passed them to Corey. "Now get dressed and we'll go." She left the room.

Corey pulled on his still-damp pants. *Oh, boy,* he

suddenly realized. *If she's taking me home, that means I'll be in her car—the red 1911 Matheson Touring car with the self-starting four-cylinder vertical engine that Dad said we'll own someday.* Someday. Corey knew "someday" would never come. But tonight Corey would get a chance to ride in that amazing car!

He imagined himself driving down Center Street in the front seat of the legendary convertible while the McDooley twins stood on the sidewalk with their mouths open.

"Come on, hurry up," Mrs. Chudzik called. "I'll wait outside." She took her dog and left.

Once he was dressed, Corey walked hesitantly out into the hallway again. He heard a low hooting sound coming from another room off to the right and stepped closer to the door.

Then another hoot—like an owl. Did she keep owls in the house? He looked around again at the dark rooms, then tiptoed to the closed door and knocked softly. "Mrs. Chudzik? Is that you?"

No answer. He put his ear to the door and heard a noise, like something scraping and clinking. *CRASH!* The door pushed open, and before Corey could take a breath, the huge beast burst out of the room and jumped on Corey, knocking him onto the floor, its tongue and teeth close to Corey's face.

"Stop!" he yelled. "Get off me!"

Almost immediately, the hairy dog and his wet tongue stopped, stepped back, and sat up pretty, like dogs are taught to do—front legs extended, with what looked like a toothy smile on his face. The dog was sitting up and grinning at Corey.

"I thought Mrs. Chudzik took you out," Corey whispered. "You scared the life out of me."

The dog understood and sat down, his tail wagging nonstop. Corey carefully put out his hand to pat the dog's head, but pulled it back quickly. The dog, however, took Corey's hand into his mouth. Corey could feel the teeth, but the teeth didn't bite. It seemed to be a friendly gesture, as if they were shaking hands. In a moment, he let go, but continued lapping Corey's hand. All the while, the tail never stopped flapping.

Mrs. Chudzik appeared at the door. "Taking all night to put on your clothes? Come on! Let's get you home." She stopped as she noticed her dog next to Corey. "Oh, I was going to leave Hovi, but I see he unlocked the door again. He does that with his teeth. I should have warned you. Hovi has a habit of doing what he thinks are good deeds. It's his nature. Now that he's saved you, he may think *you* belong to him. You'll just have to put up with it."

She pulled on the black cape over her head and arms. For a moment Corey had the vision of a large hovering bird fluttering its wings before seizing its prey.

"Come along," she ordered, beckoning him with a long finger. "You, too, Hovi."

At Mrs. Chudzik's invitation, Hovi took off instantly. He whooshed past them and jumped into the front passenger seat of the waiting touring car that hummed and glowed in the driveway.

4

The 1911 Matheson Touring Car

Corey gazed in total admiration. The full moon had risen and the bright red Matheson Touring car shone like something alive, brilliant and beautiful. It was the latest, 1911 model—and it was still 1910! Best of all, he was going to ride in it!

"Backseat, Hovi."

The dog hopped smoothly into the backseat. Mrs. Chudzik put on a huge pair of driving goggles and adjusted them. Although they were meant to keep out dust and bugs, they looked more like magnifying lenses. Her eyes bulged even larger in the goggles.

She reached over and opened the passenger side door. "Don't stand there gawking. Hop in."

"Oh, okay, sure." Corey climbed in the front seat, hoping Hovi didn't mind. But Hovi sat happily in the rear, waiting for the ride to start.

Mrs. Chudzik backed the car out of the driveway and onto the street. The headlights were as bright as a train's, and the engine purred as quietly as a cat.

Corey spoke up. "Thanks, Mrs. Chudzik. I always wanted to have a ride in this . . ."

"Chariot. I call it my chariot."

"It sure is a nice chariot," Corey said.

"Now, where do you live?" she asked.

Corey recited his address and sat back in the soft leather seat. "This feels good on my sore back."

"I must have worked on you for an hour doing artificial respiration. I probably broke a few of your ribs," Mrs. Chudzik said as her chariot glided down the hilly streets. "My back is hurting too. Bending over you for an hour isn't something I should be doing at my age."

They passed by a clock that said 10:25, and he began to think about his mom and dad. Mom would be crying, and Dad would be checking with all the neighbors and pacing the streets looking for him. He hadn't told Mom about going skating, as she had gone shopping. He should have left a note.

"My mom will be upset—she had no idea I was going skating," he confided to Mrs. Chudzik. "And my dad will be worried and probably mad at me."

"I imagine so," Mrs. Chudzik agreed, nodding. "I never had children, but when my husband was alive and working as a doctor, I could easily see how many parents have their hearts broken by thoughtless children—or sick children who die—not that *they* could help it. I'm glad I didn't have any children. They only bring heartbreak."

Corey didn't want to bring heartbreak to his mom and dad. He tried hard to hold back tears, but they slipped silently down his cheeks anyway. "Can you speed up a little?"

Mrs. Chudzik was already traveling at a brisk twenty miles per hour. "No. I didn't spend an hour doing artificial respiration only to have you die in an accident."

Corey sighed and blinked his eyes. The lights in the town blurred as tears kept coming.

They turned onto Corey's street, which was part of a patch village owned by the Mountain Crest Mine Company, where his dad was a miner. The houses lined the road and most looked alike, with rickety wooden porches on the front.

In the backyards were gardens where the families grew vegetables. The village looked something like a patchwork quilt with the squares of grassy lawns in the front of the house and the little blocks of gardens in the back.

"My house is the one with the nice stone porch on the front."

"Where? They all look alike. What number is your house?"

"Forty-five."

"Still hard to see the number. Why does anyone put up tiny numbers and then hide them somewhere?" Mrs. Chudzik muttered, slowing down.

"There it is." Home had never looked as good to Corey as it did right then. The tightness in his chest loosened at the sight of the lighted windows in his house. The porch was alight too, with lanterns, and the front door was open. Lots of people were inside, and Corey could see a police wagon—a Black Maria—parked out front.

"They're all looking for you," Mrs. Chudzik said. "As much as I hate meeting people, I suppose I'll have to get out and explain what happened." She pulled in behind the Black Maria.

"Oh yes, please," Corey said, nodding vigorously. "I can't explain this all by myself." He had the door of the car open before she turned off the engine.

Someone looked out the front door and yelled, "It's Mrs. Chudzik's car . . . and, oh my Lord—it's Corey. He's here!"

He could hear his brothers, Jack and Sammy, calling out, "Corey's back, Corey's back!"

Hovi jumped out and waited for Corey, and then as Corey headed toward the house, the dog trotted close to his side.

The light in the doorway dimmed as several people clustered together, looking out. "Corey?" "Is that you, Corey?" "What happened?" A dozen questions.

"Mom! Dad!" He raced onto the walk and bolted up the front steps two by two with the big dog at his heels.

Mom was on the porch, her hair undone, and her face swollen from crying. "Corey!" she wailed, clutching him. "Where have you been?" She burst into tears as she kissed his cheeks, and hair, and eyes. "Oh, Corey, we were so frightened."

Dad pulled him away from his mother and shook him by the shoulders. "Where have you been? What happened? Didn't you even think how upset your mother would be?"

Hovi growled. He did not like Dad shaking Corey. Dad let go and looked down at the dog. "Who is this?"

"It's Hovi. He saved me." Corey tried to say more, but everyone was talking and questioning him, and then, in the midst of it all, Mrs. Chudzik came up onto the porch.

"He very nearly drowned," she said in her deep voice. "He was skating on the pond down by my home, when the ice gave way."

Silence reigned as everyone crowded the small porch to listen to Mrs. Chudzik, who stood there like a foreign dignitary—tall, aloof, head high—among the coal miners and their needy families.

Corey nodded. "I was drowned. I felt my feet touch the bottom, under the ice, and I couldn't find my way out. The ice was hard, like a roof above me."

"So how did you get out?" Dad asked.

"Hovi, my dog, was tied up down by the pond. He began barking madly. He actually pulled free of his chain and came rushing up to the house, howling like a wild animal." Mrs. Chudzik smiled slightly. "He was insistent that I follow him down to the pond." She patted Hovi's head. "In fact, he has adopted Corey, I think."

"Mrs. Chudzik, I shudder to think what could have happened if it weren't for your wonderful dog—our little boy would be dead," Aunt Millie gushed, and wrung her hands.

"Yes, indeed he would," Mrs. Chudzik agreed. "However, as Hovi continued racing back and forth, trying to tell me, I saw the hole in the ice, and I figured out what had happened. I grabbed a rake and raced down to the pond. I was able to chop away the ice around the hole, until I could see him on the bottom. I then reached down with the rake and tugged at his coat until I could grab hold, bring him up, and pull him out."

Everyone on the porch—and on the neighbors' porches two houses down on either side—strained to hear the story. When she paused, the chattering and questions started again. However, some of the neighbors didn't speak at all but cowered nearby, nudging one another at Mrs. Chudzik's terrifying narrative.

"She's enough to scare any kid to death," someone murmured. "Did you see her eyes? They stare right through you."

"Hush!" Mrs. Chudzik ordered in her mannish voice. "Let me finish!" She turned her head and sent a scathing look at her audience. Immediately, everyone was silent. Then she removed her goggles, took a deep breath, and continued.

"The boy wasn't breathing, of course. I didn't know how long he'd been in the pond, so I started artificial respiration on him at once—right there on the ice."

"I don't remember anything about being rescued," Corey added.

"You could have died!" Mom cried.

"He might have been dead," Mrs. Chudzik said. "I didn't hear a heartbeat."

"Oh . . . no heartbeat," someone said. "He was dead."

"She has strange powers," another neighbor said in awe.

"Supernatural powers," Mrs. Sullivan stated with a nod.

Then Dad's booming voice carried over the neighborhood. "Corey, you should have told someone where you were."

Mrs. Chudzik waited until it was quiet again. "I bent over him and worked on him for at least . . . oh, I don't know. It is hard to pay attention to time when you're trying to resuscitate someone. It must have been a half hour before he started breathing again and upchucked that pond water. It was dark and cold by the time I brought him up to the house in the wheelbarrow." Several folks chuckled.

"Lucky it was there," she said with a scowl at those who laughed. "I have been working on the drainage from my house to the pond, and I happened to have the wheelbarrow nearby in the bushes. I couldn't have carried him up the hill without it." After a respectful silence from her chastised audience, Mrs. Chudzik continued, "I put him to bed with hot water bottles. I had no idea who he was, so even if I'd had a telephone, I wouldn't have known whom to call. Besides, I had to rest in the parlor myself until he came in and woke me."

"She was lying in a . . . ," he started to say, but stopped when he saw the look Mrs. Chudzik gave him.

"He seems to be fine now," she said after a moment. "Keep him warm and in bed for a few days." She headed toward the porch steps. "You need to watch his cough. It could develop into pneumonia."

Gasps came from the audience. Pneumonia was often a death sentence.

"Mrs. Chudzik, how can we thank you?" Mom touched the woman's shoulder. "Please stay and have some hot chicken soup . . . or something . . . tea?"

"Another time," Mrs. Chudzik said. "And, Corey, you come see me when you are over this close call with death. I'll be interested in knowing how you are."

"I will, Mrs. Chudzik, I will." Corey went over to her and put his arms around her. "Thank you." He could feel her stiffen as he hugged her.

"Enough of that." She shoved him away, whistled loudly for Hovi, and then the two of them climbed into her beautiful chariot. Hovi looked sadly at Corey but climbed dutifully into the front seat.

Mrs. Chudzik put her goggles on, then raised her hand and gave a short wave.

"Thank you," came the calls.

The chattering and exclamations started again. "Well, Corey is lucky to be alive. We might never have known what happened if he'd drowned."

"Lucky for him, that dog warned Mrs. Chudzik," said Aunt Millie.

"Humph! It's a wonder the dog didn't tear him apart. Imagine, being alone in a house with that Polish woman and her vicious dog. Corey is lucky, all right," Mrs. O'Brian said with a sniff.

"She's a mean woman . . . and ugly as a witch. Did you hear her tell us to be quiet? Who does she think she is, anyway—just because she lives up there in that big house . . . ?"

"She probably is a witch. She sure enough looks like one. . . ."

"And who knows what kind of curse she might have put on Corey." Mrs. McDooley shook her head sadly. "Only time will tell the outcome of this on that boy."

"Poor Corey, up there in that house with that awful Polish woman and that coffin they say is in her parlor. And that fiend of a dog . . ."

"The family will need to keep a close watch on Corey, all right," Mrs. O'Brian agreed with a wise nod. "No tellin' what spell she may have cast on him."

Corey put his hands over his ears. He didn't want to hear anything more. "I want to go to bed now," he whispered to his mother.

So Mom brought him up to bed, got him into warm pajamas, and fed him hot chicken soup that Corey found out later had been made by Mrs. Balaski from next door.

"We mining folks stand together in bad times and good times," he heard someone say.

5
The Dreams

Boys!" Mom called to Corey's brothers. "You'll need to sleep in the parlor tonight—on the floor, or on the couch. Corey needs the bed to himself for now."

Jack, who was a few years younger than Corey, complained loudly and threw his nightshirt across the room. "We never get any sleep when we have the couch. We'll be awake all night and we'll fall asleep at school tomorrow."

Sammy, two years younger than Jack, chimed in. "It's not our fault Corey went skating on thin ice." He stuck his tongue out at his brother.

"Quiet!" Dad's loud voice boomed for silence. "Corey's constant coughing will keep you awake. We don't want the three of you up all night; then no one will get any rest. No more complaining about sleeping in the parlor. Understand?"

The boys' bedroom was on the third floor—an unfinished room with one iron bed. The three boys always slept together, sideways on the bed. Tonight, though, Corey had the entire bed to himself. This was a good deal, and it might work even longer. Hadn't Mrs. Chudzik said he needed to rest for a few days? A few days! Not bad.

Corey coughed several times and his mother rushed over to him carrying a jar. "Mrs. Sullivan told me to use this on your chest." She read the label. "Vick's. It's something new for croup and pneumonia." She unbuttoned his shirt and rubbed the gooey salve all over his chest.

"It smells strong," Corey said, inhaling the fumes.

"It's full of good things like . . ." She looked again at the label. "Menthol—which is mint, actually. You like mint, don't you? And euca . . . lyptus, and camphor. Inhale it, Corey. It'll help you breathe." She then buttoned him up, pulled an itchy woolen afghan over him, and tucked him into the blankets.

The next morning, Dad informed the school that Corey was done—finished. He would be working in the mine soon, and there was no need to go back to school. Corey felt a huge sense of relief when he knew he didn't have to face his teacher, Miss O'Shea, anymore. She didn't like or encourage children of miners. She often referred to them as "foreigners" and "ignorant."

Corey couldn't restrain himself one day when he heard her use those words. So he raised his hand, stood up, and suggested that unless someone in the room was a Native American, then everyone, including Miss O'Shea, was a foreigner.

Corey stretched out that night on the bed all by himself and fell asleep within minutes. His dreams were the shadowy rooms in Mrs. Chudzik's house; the beautiful 1911 touring car; Hovi, the dog who'd rescued him; and the coffin.

Then his dream turned to the shining ice, sparkling in the sunlight—smooth as a mirror. He skated amazingly well on the surface—better than he had ever skated. But now the ice became dark. He could feel himself sinking into the blackness of the pond—down, down into the murky water. Again he was struggling to find the hole where the ice had given way—where he could find air . . . he must find air . . . he needed to breathe. He felt his feet—with his skates still on—hit the bottom of the pond. The ice was now a roof over his head as he struggled to find his way out. He gasped and could feel the water coming into his mouth and throat . . . and he was deep in the black water . . . drowning again.

Corey screamed and woke up thrashing, coughing and gasping for air.

"Corey, it's all right. You're safe." It was his mother's voice, and he found himself in her arms.

✣ ✣ ✣

The next morning, when Corey came down for breakfast, his brothers were already at the table. They looked up from their bowls of cereal but were silent as Corey joined them. They'd probably heard his cries during the night and pestered Mom into revealing his nightmare. She must have insisted they say nothing.

The winter vacation had ended, and his brothers would be going back to school, so Corey wouldn't have to answer their questions today, or see them whispering behind their hands about his shrieks in the night. However, he was sure they'd be telling his school friends what had happened. He hoped everything would be forgotten soon.

As for Corey, he couldn't forget. That night, he had the dream again. Instead of screaming, Corey jolted awake, in a cold sweat and vomiting. After Mom had cleaned him up, it was a long time before he stopped shaking. He was afraid to sleep—even when he was drowsy and the pillow felt cool and soft.

How long would he relive, over and over again, those horrific, real moments when he was drowning?

Because of the awful dreams, Corey was allowed to have the room to himself for a while longer. His brothers were not happy with this arrangement.

"It's not fair," Sammy whined.

"He's just pretending to have those dreams so he can sleep alone," Jack insisted.

"Be kind and patient with your brother," Mom whispered. "He had a terrible ordeal. Mrs. Chudzik says he really drowned that day at the pond."

Consequently, Corey was alone in the bed, alone in the room, and for another week he lay there at night, trying not to sleep, trying to think of happy things, trying to do the times tables in his head, and then, utterly exhausted, he would fall into a deep sleep or end up back in the dark pond again.

Finally, he said to his mother, "Mom, I don't want to sleep alone anymore. Perhaps having the boys in bed with me will help me to sleep." And it did for a while.

6

The Company Store

In a few weeks, Corey was feeling well enough to take a walk up to meet his friends coming home from school. He wanted to talk with Anthony, his best friend, who would also be leaving school to work in the mine soon. A month or two ago, before Corey drowned, Dad took Corey and Anthony down into the mine to see how the nippers work—a job that sometimes came up for boys. Corey wondered if Anthony had decided to work as a nipper. He didn't want to tell Anthony about his dreams. How could he expect Anthony to understand, when he didn't understand himself?

Corey walked quickly up the unpaved roads until he reached the company store. Then he stopped, out of breath. He'd wait here until Anthony came. He was tired and sleepy and wondered how long it would be that he'd have those awful drowning nightmares. Besides, it was embarrassing for a boy of twelve to be afraid of dreams.

All the kids going home from school had to pass by the store. Some stopped and bought candy and things. Others just hung around and waited for friends. Corey figured Anthony would probably show up in a few minutes.

Meanwhile, Corey decided to take a look inside the store. A bell rang as Corey went inside and looked at the candies for sale. The name HERSHEY stood out in large letters. One whole section of the display was for Hershey's chocolates. Hershey was fast becoming a famous name in chocolate around the country, and it was manufactured right there in Pennsylvania. The chocolate candy bars were a nickel. Corey felt in his pockets and came up with four pennies.

"Do you want something?" asked the man behind the counter.

"Yes, I want a Hershey's bar, but I only have four cents."

"Well, get some penny candy," the salesclerk suggested. "There's plenty of that."

"But I really wanted a Hershey's bar."

"Why aren't you in school?"

Corey thought for a moment. "I don't go to school," he said. "I work in the mine." It wasn't really a lie. He would be working in another month or so.

"Are you twelve yet? You have to be twelve now to work down in the mine."

"I am twelve," he said. He would be twelve tomorrow,

so that was not really a lie either. Corey didn't expect any celebration. The family couldn't afford Christmas, so a birthday most likely would not be celebrated either.

"Well, now, that's different. Do you have an account here? It will make it a lot easier for you to buy things if you have an account, you know."

"No, I don't have an account, but I'd like one." It sounded grown-up to have an account of his own.

"I'll set you up right now." He took out a pad of paper. "What's your name?"

"Corey Adamski."

"Joe Adamski's kid?"

"Yes. Do you know my dad?"

"Of course I know him. He shops here a lot."

Corey remembered Mom and Dad arguing about the company store the other night. Mom was worried about bills and money, as usual. Did they owe money to the company store? He couldn't remember, exactly. "Maybe I should ask my father first."

"If you had an account in your own name right now, you could get that Hershey's bar you want, plus a few other things. You don't have to ask your father."

That sounded like a good idea. "Okay. Sign me up and I'll get that Hershey's bar for a start." Corey thought about his little brothers, Jack and Sammy, and decided he would get them something. He picked out two more Hershey's bars. Then he saw a whistle with a cord to wear around the neck, so he took two of those for his brothers. Their family hadn't given anything to one another for Christmas because there was no money. This way, at least the boys would have a present. So what if it was Corey's birthday? It was a nice idea for Corey to celebrate by giving gifts to others—sort of a good deed.

He was about to leave when he remembered Mom and Dad. He would surprise them with a gift too. He could pay for it once he started work at the mine. He looked around and found a pair of woolen socks for Dad, and a pretty box of Cashmere Bouquet Soap in the shape of shells for Mom. So far his bill came to two dollars and thirty-five cents.

Then he spotted a small leather purse—just the right size to hold change and fit into a man's back pocket. He bought three: one for Dad, one for his friend Anthony, and one for himself. They were real leather and pretty expensive at fifty cents each. The salesclerk added up the bill, which now came to three dollars and eighty-five cents.

Corey signed his name to a slip for that amount, put the bill in his pocket, took his package, and went outside.

That was easy, he thought. *Once I start working, I'll pay the bill. Mom and Dad don't need to know how I paid for it.*

He looked around to see if Anthony was coming. Instead he spotted Abby Russell in the center of a group of boys. Corey had known Abby since first grade. She was thrashing her fists and punching them as they tossed something back and forth among themselves. Her brown curly hair peeked out from her cap and bounced in the scuffle.

It looked as though the boys had something of hers and she was trying to get it. As he approached, he could see they were swinging her handbag around on its drawstring and just out of reach from Abby's hands. "Give it to me now!" she yelled, kicking the boys, her face flushed.

"Hey, what's goin' on?" Corey asked, heading their way.

"Abby got us all in trouble," Tommy McDooley answered. "We hid her purse and she told the principal."

"Why do you want a girl's purse?" Corey said with a smirk.

"We don't want one," Tommy's twin brother, Jimmy, snapped. "Are you tryin' to be funny?"

"No wonder you got in trouble. Boys are not supposed to touch girls' pocketbooks," Corey stated.

"Since when did you care about rules?" Tommy asked.

"I don't care anymore 'cause I'm through with school. I'm starting work in the mine soon." Corey could see Abby's eyes on her purse, which still dangled just above her head. "For Pete's sake, just give Abby her purse."

"Why don't you go on home and mind your own business," Red O'Brian said, giving Corey a shove.

"Yeah, Corey, go on home. Quit bossin' us around," Jimmy added.

"He thinks since he's a workin' man now, he can tell us what to do," Red said with a sneer.

"Workin' man? He's heading into the mines and won't come out until there's a Black Maria waitin' for him. He'll never amount to anything but a coal miner," Jimmy added.

"What's wrong with bein' a coal miner? My dad's a coal

miner, and so is yours. Didn't they amount to anything?" Corey demanded.

"Don't you say anything about our dad," Jimmy warned.

"Our dad won't let *us* quit school to work in the mine," Tommy said.

Corey didn't feel like arguing. "I'm goin' home, where I don't have to deal with you *kids* anymore." He turned on his heel and headed in the other direction. "Leave Abby alone. Go buy your own purse and quit picking on her."

"We'll get you later, Abby." Tommy threw Abby's purse at her and the boys walked off.

Abby retrieved her purse from the street, brushed it off, and ran to catch up with Corey. "Thanks, Corey," she said breathlessly.

"Have you seen Anthony?" Corey asked her.

Abby straightened her hat, looked over her shoulder, and pointed. "There he is now, coming around the bend."

Anthony was meandering along the street, kicking at a stone here and there, but when he looked up and saw Corey and Abby, he ran toward them. "Hey, Corey, where have you been?"

"I've been sick," Corey answered.

Anthony caught up with Corey and Abby and they all walked together up the street toward home. "I heard you nearly drowned."

"Not *nearly*. I *did* drown. I was dead until Mrs. Chudzik and her dog saved me."

"Mrs. Chudzik and her dog saved you? Wow," Anthony said. "Did you get to go inside her house? Did you see anything?"

"What do you mean?" Corey asked.

"Did you see any signs of . . . bones or torture chambers?"

"You mean like the stories about her luring kids into her home and then they are never heard from again?" Corey asked.

"Yeah, things like that—those kinds of stories." Anthony leaned closer. "Corey, it could have been you. You could have been taken and no one would know where you were. Mama said you probably had a curse put on you."

"Well, nothin' happened like that," Corey told him.

Abby rolled her eyes. "It was a good thing that it was Mrs. Chudzik who saved him. She was a doctor, you know. My dad said she studied medicine in Switzerland under a famous Polish woman doctor, Anna Tomaszewicz-Dobrska. Imagine that. A girl growing up to be a doctor."

"I thought only boys were doctors," Anthony said. "Girls become nurses."

"Well, Mrs. Chudzik is a doctor. Even though she doesn't have her license to practice medicine, she is a registered nurse here in Pennsylvania."

"How do you know so much about her?" Corey asked.

"She lives next door to us. I know enough about her not to believe those stupid rumors."

"So she's a doctor *and* a nurse. Then I was lucky to have

her save me, wasn't I?" Corey said. "But she and her dog are pretty scary just the same."

No one spoke for a while, and then Anthony asked, "What does she look like? You must have seen her close up. I heard she has a beak. Does she? And what about the whiskers on her chin?"

"Her nose is pointy—kind of like a beak," Corey said. "I don't think she could crack nuts with it or anything. It's just . . . big and sharp."

"What about the whiskers?"

"I didn't notice whiskers, but she has huge black eyes. I'll bet she could turn a person to stone when she's angry."

Anthony stopped walking. "Really? What about her voice? Does she sound like a witch?"

"I don't know what a witch sounds like," Corey admitted. "But she does shriek. She shrieks at people and talks over them—especially when she's mad."

"You saw her mad? Really?" Anthony asked. "Did anyone turn to stone?

"No, of course not! She just told the neighbors to shut up when she was talking," Corey answered. That was true, he thought. She *did* shriek. And everyone *did shut up.*

"They were probably rude to her," Abby said. "She had a good reason to tell them to shut up."

"She never used those exact words, though," Corey said, feeling guilty. "She more or less waited until they were quiet."

They had arrived at the crossroads to Corey's patch. Corey was about to head home but changed his mind. "I'll walk a little way with you." He turned to Anthony and said, "I wondered if you had decided to be a nipper."

"No! I would be bored to death, sittin' around waitin' to open or close the door for the coal cars on their way to the breaker. And if you didn't open the door soon enough . . . POW! The whole carload of coal would crash through, and probably squash you to death," Anthony said.

"Besides, I hear it's lonely bein' a nipper, sitting by yourself and waiting for those cars to come rolling down," Corey added.

"That nipper Freddie had a butty," Anthony said with a grin at Abby. "A big rat. He tamed it by giving him bits of his lunch every day."

"Some miners toss scraps from their lunches to the knockers every night when they leave the mine," Corey said. "That food disappears."

"Sure it disappears. The rats eat it," Anthony said.

"Oh, that's creepy," Abby said. "Between the stories I've heard about the knockers or the rats, I think I prefer the rats."

"You don't believe the tales about the knockers, do you?" Corey asked.

"Well, who's to say?" Abby said. "People have actually seen the rats, but who has ever seen a knocker? I don't believe in any of those silly tales. They're like the stories we hear about Mrs. Chudzik and her dog. They're just not true."

"From what Corey said, the stories about Mrs. Chudzik are true," Anthony answered.

"No, they're not. She was okay to me," Corey said. "She's just odd, that's all."

"Well, I do believe in the knockers," Anthony said.

"My grandpa from Wales called the knockers 'Coblynau,' and when he talked about them, they sure sounded believable," Corey agreed.

"We don't need to worry if we are breaker boys," Anthony said. "Now, that would be fun. They play baseball at lunch every day and then play other mining companies every spring. It's a big community game. I wouldn't mind that." He turned to Corey and shook his head. "I'm pretty good as a pitcher."

"It would be fun to get on a baseball team," Corey said. "My dad pitches to me and I smash some of the balls right out of sight."

"I don't know how the breaker boys can pitch or hold a bat," Abby said. "They have terrible cuts on their hands from the coal and the slate. Their hands bleed and are all covered with pus and . . . sometimes they lose a finger—or even a hand."

"Losing a finger won't kill you." Anthony scoffed. "That's nothin'."

Abby shuddered and shook her head. "Oh yes, it is *something*. What would you do if you lost your finger?"

The boys looked at each other and shrugged. "We'll be all right if we're careful," Corey told her.

"Besides, it hardly ever happens," Anthony added.

"You hope so. I've heard what happened to the McGregor boy who fell into the machinery at the breaker and was crushed to a pulp," Abby said. "Can't you find anything else to do at the mine?"

"Corey's dad said he'd take us down to see about being mule drivers," Anthony said. He turned to Corey. "When will we go, Corey? Has your dad mentioned it lately?"

"No, we haven't talked about it since my accident. I almost had pneumonia, you know." He coughed for effect.

Abby's jaw dropped. "That would have been awful!" she exclaimed.

"Well, you didn't get pneumonia, did you?" Anthony asked.

"No, but I could have."

"Driving a mule can be dangerous too," Abby said. "Mules are ornery. If they don't like you, they can corner you in a stall and then stomp on you. I've heard terrible stories about mules."

"I wouldn't mind being a mule driver," Corey said.

"Mules are more dangerous than—" Abby started.

"Abby, stop it!" Anthony ordered. "You're gettin' on our nerves."

"Well, my father is an engineer at the mine, and he knows things going on that you don't ever hear about," Abby sputtered angrily.

"Forget it, Abby. Anthony and I have to work. We have to help our families. So don't tell us all the gloomy stories you've heard. It doesn't help us one bit," Corey said.

"Any work in the mine is dangerous," Anthony said to Abby, "but Corey and I can handle it."

They walked along for a while with no one speaking.

Corey felt a bit sorry, as he saw Abby's grumpy expression, her lips turned down in an angry pout. Abby had a hard time at school. Girls didn't like her because her father wasn't a miner but a professional engineer, and that gave her a different status from most of the girls. The boys always picked on her, but Corey thought that was because she was pretty and nice and they probably really liked her but would never admit it.

The trio approached Anthony's road, which led down to another patch village owned by the mining company. The houses were older and shabbier than Corey's, and outhouses were lined up on a long stretch of grass in the middle of the street for the families to share.

"Oh, I forgot, Anthony. I bought you something." Corey set down the company store bag he was carrying and pulled out the coin purse. "This is for you. I thought you could use it when you start work. I got one for my dad and for me, too. It's real leather."

Anthony took the leather purse and turned it over and over in his hand. "Hey, this is real nice of you, Corey. Thanks a lot."

"You're welcome," Corey said. "See you later."

"Bye, Corey. Bye, Abby." Anthony turned and raced down the road to his house.

Corey and Abby continued up the road without speaking for a while. Then Corey said, "I'm sorry I yelled at you."

"It's okay. I'm sure you and Anthony already know the dangers at the mine."

"We'll be careful. We don't *want* to get hurt, you know."

"I'll be turning off here. It's my shortcut." Abby nodded toward the woods. "No one uses this path very often. I've been going home this way so I don't have to deal with those boys who take my purse all the time. I don't want them to know where I live."

Corey could barely see the trail, which wound its way through the woods. Patches of melting snow still lingered in the shaded areas. No one would ever realize there was a path there. "So, this little track must lead to Mrs. Chudzik's house too."

"Yes, it goes right down to her back door and off to our house."

"Good to know," Corey said, making a mental note.

"I feel sorry for Mrs. Chudzik. People talk about her and kids are mean to her."

"She's strange, but she saved my life," Corey said. "Have you ever been in her parlor?"

"No. Have you?" Abby asked.

Corey told Abby how he woke up in Mrs. Chudzik's house, after drowning, and how he found Mrs. Chudzik in the coffin.

Abby opened her mouth in astonishment. "What? She was lying in a coffin? In her parlor?"

Corey nodded. "Abby, please don't say anything to anyone. Mrs. Chudzik did save my life, and I don't want to pay her back by telling her secret. I probably shouldn't have told you—about the coffin, I mean. And I probably said too much to Anthony."

"I won't tell anyone, Corey. She was wonderful to have saved you."

"Actually, her dog, Hovi, saved me by barking and taking her down to the pond."

"Her dog petrifies me, especially his bark."

"He saved me, and now he thinks I belong to him." Corey laughed. "He jumps and laps my face when he sees me."

"I wouldn't want those teeth near my face. Thanks for walking with me, Corey," Abby said before running off onto the hidden trail. "Bye!" she called as she disappeared into the shadows of the trees.

7
Into the Mine

As usual, Corey didn't sleep much that night. He tried to stay awake, turning and tossing until the blanket was tangled, and Sammy yelled at him. He fought sleep in a dozen ways, reciting the times tables way beyond twelves, but he found his mind wandering. He forced himself to stay awake so he wouldn't dream—and he was drowsy when Mom came in to get him up early next morning.

"Dad said you'd be going with him today to see if you and Anthony might be mule drivers. Dad talked with Anthony's father yesterday, so Anthony will meet you at the mine." Mom sounded excited for him—as if she was counting on him and was sure that things would be better now.

She and Corey went downstairs, where Dad waited,

finishing up a mug of coffee. "How do you feel this morning?" Dad asked.

"I'm okay," Corey answered. He sat at the table and tried not to show how sleepy he was. He was worried about going into the mine and he didn't feel at all hungry.

Then, after Mom packed the lunch pails, Dad and Corey kissed her good-bye. "Good luck, Corey. I hope you get a job. I'm not sure how you'll do with a mule, but whatever you do, I know you will be a good worker and a big help to our family." She sounded cheerful, but Corey could see tears brighten her eyes.

He and his dad started their hike up the road toward the coal mine. It was still dark and took over a half hour to walk up the hill to the Mountain Crest mine. As they approached, other miners, breaker boys, and workers joined them. By the time they reached the mine, a long line of workers had arrived at the mine and breaker. Their voices, along with the morning whistle, and the nearby locomotive on its way to the canal with its load of coal, all made strange music in the morning air.

Dad took Corey to the office, where Anthony was already waiting. "Corey is back again, and eager to work in the mine," Dad told Mr. McBride, one of the supervisors. "The boys are interested in becoming mule drivers."

"We do have an opening for one mule driver coming up soon, and there will be more jobs available once the new mules come in from Tennessee. Why don't I take you boys down to the stables. There may be some drivers grooming and feeding their mules down there—that's part of the job, you know. The mule drivers love their mules, as you've probably heard. But it takes a bit of work to get used to the job—and to the mules." Mr. McBride stood up and signaled for Corey and Anthony to follow him. "Come along."

"I'll come too," Dad said. "You're going my way anyhow."

"Oh, that's right. You're working on that new shaft—what do you call it?"

"The North Star Chamber," Dad answered. "It heads due north. We're quite a way into the mountain now. We'll be dynamiting again soon. I found a big vein of anthracite that needs to be opened up."

The two men, with Corey and Anthony a few steps behind, went to where the empty coal cars rolled down deep into the mine, to be refilled with coal. "Since this car is empty and ready to go back, we'll ride in this, instead of taking the elevator cage," Mr. McBride suggested.

"Keep your heads down, boys," Dad warned. "In some places you'll only be a few inches under the rock ceiling."

"It would be a bad blow if you hit your head," Mr. McBride agreed as they climbed in.

They crouched as the coal car began its swift trip down the tracks with the stone roof just inches above them. The darkness gathered, and Corey noticed the various shades of blackness as they descended deeper into the earth. The excitement and adventure he felt at first quickly gave way to uneasiness, and then dread. The ceiling in the downhill shaft was flashing by close above their heads.

"Hey, this is fun!" Anthony yelled.

Corey didn't think it was fun. He was feeling sick, and even though the mine was cold, Corey was sweating. He struggled to take off his coat.

"Keep your coat on, Corey," Dad ordered. "You don't have room to take it off."

Corey hardly heard his father's voice. The rhythmic knocking of the cart on the tracks reminded Corey of the stories his Welsh grandfather told him about the Coblynau, the evil elves who live in the mines, waiting to cause disaster.

Clank! Clank! Clank! The sound gave Corey a headache. The clicking wheels and the momentum as the car careened down the shaft, the rock walls that flew by in a blur, and the black hole into which they were descending were all that Corey could now hear or see. He was dizzy and sick to his stomach. If he could just remove his hot jacket . . . He pulled at his coat frantically, ripping the buttons off.

I've got to get out of here. I can't breathe. Corey got to his knees and then tried to stand and escape the terrifying descent into the abyss.

"Corey! No!" shouted his father. "Stay down!"

"You'll smash your brains out!" Mr. McBride yelled. But Corey seemed unaware of the danger. Then, as the car dove under another narrow ceiling, Mr. McBride threw himself across Corey and pinned him to the floor of the coal car.

✣ ✣ ✣

When he awoke, Corey was in the makeshift first aid room in the mine. He was resting on a cot, and his father stood over him, pale as a ghost. Mr. McBride was gone, but Corey remembered the mine boss throwing himself on top of him—and that was all he could recall.

He sat up and looked at his father. "I'm sorry, Dad," he whispered, and then hung his head. "I couldn't help it. It was just like my dreams. I was drowning and I had to get out—I had to escape from that stone ceiling and get air."

Anthony peeked in from outside the room. "Are you okay now, Corey?"

"I'm fine," Corey answered, but his voice trembled.

"You'll be fine," Dad assured him. "Mr. McBride pushed you down just in time."

"I spoiled everything, didn't I?" Corey asked tearfully. "Are you ashamed of me, Dad?"

"It's my fault for bringing you down here. I never thought the dream would come back while you were *awake*." Dad sat next to Corey on the cot and put his arm around Corey's shoulders. "Are you all right now? Or do you need to get out of the mine?"

Corey looked around the room. The stone walls and ceiling had been painted white to look like a hospital room. It didn't make any difference. The cold harshness of the mine was still all around him, pressing him in. "Dad, please get me out of here."

"Come on." Dad helped Corey off the cot, and they headed out into the gangway—the working center of the mine, where Anthony was waiting.

"It's okay, Corey," Anthony said. "We can see the mules some other time."

Corey still felt the mine closing in on him as he entered the great chamber. He closed his eyes as the choking feeling started again.

"Keep your eyes closed, and I'll lead you. The elevator to bring you to the surface is not far away. Just concentrate on my voice," Dad told him.

Corey stumbled along as Dad pulled him across the stony floor, with Anthony following. "My head is hurting," he mumbled to Anthony. "I have to close my eyes." Did Anthony understand what had happened?

He heard familiar sounds—a mule's strange whinny somewhere nearby, wheels of a coal car, men's voices, and the clanking of picks and shovels as miners dug into the walls. He hoped no one could see him being led by his father like a scared little kid.

"You'll be up out of the mine soon," Dad said, helping Corey into the cage that would bring him to the surface.

Corey opened his eyes briefly to see he was being pulled up. It wasn't fast, like the coal car he had come down in. Instead, it made its way slowly up to the daylight above. He knew that Anthony stood silently nearby in the cage, probably wondering what was wrong with Corey.

When Corey felt the sunlight envelop him, he relaxed, knowing he was no longer under the earth. Corey gave his friend a weak smile, and Anthony grinned and nodded.

"You'll be all right, Corey," Dad whispered. "Do you want to go home now?"

"Yes, I want to go home."

"How about you, Anthony?"

"I'll stay for a while. Mr. McBride says he'll show me around the stables, and then I can eat lunch with my dad."

"That's a great idea," Dad agreed. "You can tell Corey all about it."

Corey really wanted to see the mules—not just to hear about them from Anthony. New mules were coming soon, Mr. McBride had said. This would be the time to make a decision and even get his own mule that he would care for and ride. It would belong to the mining company, of course, but he heard that the drivers loved their mules and felt ownership of them, and the mules felt the same way.

However, the mules all lived in their stables down in the mine. Corey knew that he could never go down into the mine again.

8
Accusations

Corey hardly noticed the long walk. He dreaded explaining to Mom, who'd said just this morning that she was counting on him, that he'd failed his family and couldn't work down in the mine after all.

He was relieved when he looked behind and saw his father running to catch up with him. "I thought I should be with you to explain to Mom what happened," Dad said breathlessly. "You had a tough day. I guess it's going to take more time for you to get over almost drowning."

Was Corey imagining disappointment in Dad's voice? "I'm awful sorry, Dad."

"It's been a month," Dad said. "You should be over this by now."

"I don't want to talk about it," Corey said.

"Corey, you don't have to give in to those feelings," Dad said. He put his arm around Corey's shoulder. "Be brave and fight the fear. You'll get over it."

Corey kicked a stone. *Dad thinks I'm not brave. He thinks I give in and don't fight. He just doesn't understand.*

As they turned into their patch, Dad found a ball on the side of the road. "Run ahead and we can pitch a few back and forth."

Corey ran forward, and Dad pitched the ball. Corey reached up and caught it easily. They pitched back and forth until they reached their house. "You're a good catcher and pitcher, son," Dad told him. "I heard the Mountain Crest breaker boys have a good team. If you get a job at the mine, you can join them. They'll be playing for the valley championship this year. You'd like that, wouldn't you?"

"It doesn't look like I'll ever get to work for the mine after what happened today."

"Get over it, Corey," said Dad, heading into the house. "Just get over it."

Every night when Dad got home, he'd go into the kitchen to bathe. Mom would stay to scrub his back, and then, when he finished bathing, he'd come out relaxed and happy and ready to hear everyone's tale of the day.

Tonight was no different. Mom brought in the tub, filled it with hot water from the stove, and made it sudsy with soap. Then Dad closed the door. Corey knew his father had had a hard day too, all because of Corey. Dad was disappointed and worried. How could Corey help the family if he couldn't work?

It was during his bath that Dad must have told Mom what had happened at the mine today. Mom was quieter when she came out of the kitchen, and Corey figured she knew.

Corey decided that tonight, when the family was clustered in the parlor, he'd give them their surprises and cheer them up. He would feel better when he saw their happy expressions. Only he'd never explain that he had charged the gifts at the company store. *I'll find a way to pay the bill. But for now, I just want to see everyone smile and be happy.*

After Dad's bath, Corey carried the big tub out into the yard, spilling the suds along the way. Then when it was empty, he put it back in the shed. Now he was alone and able to pull out the bag full of surprises that he'd hidden yesterday when he got home.

Ah, there it was, tucked underneath the bottom shelf, exactly as he'd left it. He threw away the company store bag, then wrapped the gifts into an old towel that hung on the drying rack. Before anyone could see and ask what he was carrying, he ran through the house and up the stairs.

His brothers were still outside playing, so the bedroom was empty as he poured the items onto the bed. He looked over Mom's castile soap in the shape of shells. They were packed in a pretty box with a picture of the seashore. She could use the box for her special things after the soap was gone.

Corey was sure his brothers would be happy with the Hershey's bars and the whistles.

Dad's socks and leather coin purse were nice too. Corey couldn't wait to surprise everyone. He'd do it after supper, when everyone was relaxed. He pushed the gifts under his bed.

Later, after the dishes were done and his brothers had gone upstairs, Corey explained to Mom what happened to him in the mine.

"When I went down into the mine, I felt sick. I'll be all right, Mom. Just a little while longer and I'll go to work."

"Sure you will," Mom agreed.

"Why don't I just become a breaker boy?" Corey suggested. "They work on the breaker, not down in the mine."

Mom nodded. "We'll see."

"We'll talk about it another day," Dad said.

"Good idea," Corey agreed. "Let's not talk about the mine tonight. I have a surprise for all of you."

"A surprise?" Mom asked.

"You may have forgotten that today's my birthday. I'm twelve now, and—"

"Oh, we didn't forget, son," Dad said quickly. "It's just that . . ."

"I know, there wasn't enough money for gifts this year, but I wanted to give you all something special, just to make everyone happy and feel good for a change."

Having heard the word "surprise," Jack and Sammy

flew down the stairs. "A surprise? For us? What is it? Tell us, Corey!"

Corey went up to his bedroom and brought down the gifts. "These are for you kids," he said, handing the boys the Hershey's bars.

"Oh, we love Hershey's bars," Jack said, carefully unwrapping the paper.

Sammy ripped off the wrapper and bit into the candy. "Thanks, Corey."

"But that's not all," Corey said, passing them the two whistles.

Jack dropped the candy bar and blew the whistle over and over again.

Sammy tried the whistle, but his mouth was too full of chocolate.

"It was nice of your brother to give you the whistles," Mom said to the boys. "But please don't blow them in the house."

"And now your present, Mom." Corey smiled as he handed his mother the pretty box of soap.

"For me?" She looked at the box quizzically. "What is this? Shells?" She read the box. "Oh, it's castile soap. That's lovely, Corey. Thank you. I've never had pure castile soap in my life." She looked over at her husband.

"And here's yours, Dad." Corey handed him the socks and the change purse. "The purse is real leather."

Dad took them in his hand and turned them over and over. "Corey, where did you get the money to pay for these gifts?"

"You always told me, 'When someone gives you a gift, don't ask how much it cost. It's not polite.'"

"This soap must have been expensive," Mom said. "It's something I would never buy."

"Did you buy anything else?" Dad asked.

"Yes, I bought one of those purses for myself and one for Anthony," Corey answered.

"Where did you get the money?" Dad asked again.

Corey shifted from one foot to another and his fists tightened. "I thought you'd be happy."

"We *are* happy," Mom said quickly. "We just wonder where the money came from for you to buy us these very nice gifts."

"They only cost three or four dollars."

"Only *three* or *four* dollars!" Mom exclaimed. "Four dollars would buy enough food for a week for this family."

"You always told me not to ask how much money a gift cost."

"We need to know because you didn't have any money to spend," Mom said.

"What does it matter where I got the money? It's the thought that counts, not the price. You always say that, too." He felt hot inside as anger welled up. "I wanted to surprise you. Now you've spoiled everything."

Dad took a deep breath, put his hands on Corey's shoulders, and looked him straight in the eye. "I need to know, Corey. Did you steal these things?"

Corey couldn't speak. His mouth went dry as disbelief flooded over him. How could Dad ask such a question?

Didn't he know Corey would never take something that didn't belong to him?

"Can't you answer, Corey?" Dad continued. "Perhaps I asked the wrong question. Let me ask you this instead. Did you steal *money* to buy these things?"

Corey stared at his father as if he were a stranger. "I never stole anything in my life." He turned and ran up the stairs to the bedroom and slammed the door.

9
Trust

Corey fell onto the bed and pulled the pillow over his head to silence his sobs. He'd wanted to surprise his family with the gifts and make them smile for a change. Instead, Mom and Dad had accused him of stealing.

I'll never forgive them, Corey vowed.

He stopped crying, pushed the pillow aside, and listened. He could hear the shrill sounds of his brothers as they played with their whistles.

"Stop blowing those whistles!" Mom yelled.

"Go out on the porch," Dad ordered Jack and Sammy. "Mom and I need to talk."

I should have known whistles would drive Mom crazy. Everything bothers her, including us.

For a while, things were quiet downstairs, and Corey

wondered what was happening. Not that he cared.

He could hear muffled voices from below, and he was certain they were discussing him. Then he heard footsteps up the stairs. Corey braced himself for more questions. He'd planned to tell his parents about the company store sometime, but that would be after the bill was paid, and by then there would be no need to confess. He took a deep breath, pulled the pillow over his face, and waited.

"Corey?" A soft knock sounded on the door, and then Mom's voice. "I'm coming in."

"No. I want to be alone." He would not make this easy for either of them.

"Please, Corey. Come on," she pleaded. "We're sorry we accused you of stealing. We know you would never steal anything. Just tell us where you got the money. That's all we need to know."

"No. I will not tell you—even if you do think I stole it, which I didn't." Corey would never give in. He could hear them whispering.

"All right, you win. We won't ask you again," Mom promised. "Now may I come in?"

Corey wanted everything to be peaceful. He hated it when there were arguments in the family. "All right. But I have something to say—once and for all." He was surprised at the firmness in his own voice.

Mom came into the room. "Dad's here. Can he come in too?" she asked.

"I suppose so," Corey said. "But no more pointing

fingers at me as if I've done something wrong."

His parents came into the room, looking sheepish. "We love you, Corey," Mom said, "and we're sorry that we thought you might have—"

"Now, listen," he said, interrupting her. "If you want me to leave school and go to work every day of my life, then you've got to trust me."

"We do—" Dad started to say.

"No, you do not. You should know I've never stolen anything. You taught me right from wrong. So you'd better have faith in me."

"In other words, you won't tell us where you got the money," Dad said.

"That's right." Corey nodded. "I'd take the gifts back if I could. But I can't. So you can keep them or give them away. I don't care anymore."

Mom and Dad looked at each other. Dad just stood there as if trying to think of something to say. Mom went to Corey and sat with him on the bed. "Corey, it was sweet that you wanted to give us all gifts. We're so sorry we spoiled your surprise. We won't ask about the money again. We love you."

Corey nodded and then buried his head in her shoulder. "I love you too." He struggled to hide his tears.

Dad said, "Sorry we didn't trust you, Corey, it was just that—"

"We will not talk about it anymore," Mom interrupted in a warning voice. She gave Corey a kiss on the cheek.

Dad approached uncertainly and then put out his right hand. "It's a deal, son. All is forgiven and forgotten."

Corey shook his hand. "Remember, Dad, a deal's a deal."

10
Asking for Help

The next morning, Corey awoke with relief that the quarrel with his parents was over and he didn't have to explain where the money came from to buy the gifts.

He was still worried that perhaps he should not have opened that charge account at the company store. The clerk there knew his dad and might tell him that Corey had opened the account in his own name. What if that happened? He'd be back on the carpet with his father, who'd be mad at him for doing business on his own and all that went with it. He wished he could pay off the debt and close that account before Dad found out about it. But how could he? He had no money.

And then he needed to know why he'd felt panic in the mine—he needed help from someone.

Maybe Mrs. Chudzik knows how to stop all the dreams. After all, Abby said she was a doctor when she lived in Poland. Maybe she'll know what's wrong with me and why the dreams torment me night and day.

Yes, the only person he knew who might be able to help him with his problem was Mrs. Chudzik. But she was so scary. He recalled how she'd pulled that ugly cape on over her arms, reminding him of black wings. And when she'd peered out at him from under the hood, she'd resembled a hungry vulture, ready to pick the flesh off its victim.

Corey shook his head. He mustn't get caught up in those stories again. She had saved his life, hadn't she?

Mrs. Chudzik was a doctor and might have an idea of what to do to make Corey better. That's all he wanted—someone to talk to about his problems. Besides, she had asked him to come see her once he was better.

After breakfast, he told his mom he was going to look for work somewhere until a job as a breaker boy showed up at the mine. He headed out the door and up the street past Anthony's road until he turned into the woods at the big boulder. He followed the narrow path to the end, and just as Abby had said, he came out of the woods directly above the Chudzik mansion.

The red car in the driveway indicated that Mrs. Chudzik was home, but what would he say to her? He had no idea as he headed up the steps to the door.

He lifted the heavy brass knocker, then he took a second glance. It was the face of an ugly gargoyle that glared at him with bulging eyes. Did it resemble Mrs. Chudzik? Or was he imagining it?

Corey wanted to run away, but his hand slipped and the knocker bounced and banged loudly several times. It was too late to leave now. He was stupid to have come at all. The house brought back that horrible night when Mrs. Chudzik was in the coffin. He turned away and tiptoed toward the front steps, hoping she hadn't heard the knocker, when suddenly he tripped over his boot lacing and fell to the floor with a loud *thud*.

The dog inside howled, and the door opened. Mrs. Chudzik stood there, looking straight ahead. She didn't see Corey, down on the floor. "Who's there?"

"It's me, Mrs. Chudzik. I'm down here on the floor," he said, struggling to his feet.

Before he could continue, Hovi jumped out and hurled himself onto Corey, knocking him down again. The dog lapped Corey's face, whimpering and wiggling as Corey attempted to get to his feet. "It's okay, Hovi. It's just me."

"And who is 'just me'?" Mrs. Chudzik asked as she turned her attention to the floor. "Stand up! Come over here."

Corey did as he was told, and stood in front of the woman, who stared at his face for what seemed a long time. He wanted to run away. Instead he whispered, "It's me, Corey. Don't you recognize me?"

"Blond hair . . . brown eyes. Hmm. Yes, it's you," she answered with a nod.

"I'm sorry I made so much noise."

"Well, come inside. I'm sure you are here for something or other."

"Yes. You did ask me to come see you when I recovered from drowning . . . and also, I thought maybe I could talk to you about a problem I have. Perhaps you can help me."

"Maybe," she answered. "Maybe not."

Corey wished again he hadn't come. Mrs. Chudzik probably thought he was a nuisance. But he couldn't leave now, after she'd invited him in.

Mrs. Chudzik beckoned him down the hallway. He noticed the big double doors to the parlor had been pulled shut. At the end of the hall was a large kitchen with a round oak table and two chairs. "Sit down," she said as she took a seat on one side of the table. "Now tell me why you're here."

Corey sat opposite her and cleared his throat nervously. "I have been having bad dreams about drowning. They're so real it's like drowning all over again. I wake up screaming and sweating. Sometimes I throw up. It even happens when I'm awake."

Mrs. Chudzik listened and nodded as Corey went on.

"Today would have been my first day working in the mine, because I turned twelve yesterday. I was hoping to get a job as a mule driver, but when I got into the coal car and went speeding down the slope into the mine, that awful dream came over me—this time while I was *awake*. I panicked, and I had to get out of the coal car, so I stood up." Corey felt anxious as he related the terror he'd felt. "I probably would have been killed, but

Mr. McBride tackled me and threw me to the floor of the car. Next thing I knew, I was in the first aid room and my father was bending over me." Corey looked sadly at Mrs. Chudzik. "I can't ever go down there again. I feel so . . . stupid." He hung his head and looked at the floor, hoping Mrs. Chudzik wouldn't see he was close to tears.

"Well, you should thank the Lord you didn't get killed."

"I thought you might know . . . why I keep thinking I'm drowning . . . when I sleep and when I'm awake."

Mrs. Chudzik seemed thoughtful for a while. Then she drew herself up and said, "Sometimes, when a person has had a frightening experience, the brain retains all the memories. Then, when something reminds the brain— with a smell or sight or whatever—the person will react as if the experience is happening all over again. It's known as 'anxiety hysteria' or a 'phobia.'"

Corey didn't quite understand, but the calm way Mrs. Chudzik explained it made him feel better. Whatever he had, it was *real*, and it had a name. *Phobia.*

"When you nearly drowned, your brain recorded the incident, so whenever something reminds you of what happened that day, your brain thinks it is happening again and it wants you be afraid—to save yourself. Doctors are beginning to understand how these phobias come about. Some people are frightened of dogs, cats, bats, birds, snakes. . . ."

"I'm not afraid of those things."

"Because you weren't threatened by them," Mrs.

Chudzik explained. "Your brain wasn't set to react by them. Instead, you react when you feel closed in, like when you fell under the ice and couldn't find your way out. The ice above was like a ceiling that held you down and you were trapped."

"Yes, yes. That's exactly how I felt in the mine yesterday."

"Anyone who went through near drowning could be afraid of the water, or being shut in under a roof, like the ice. Now that you know what causes it, it might help to remember that the fear you have of drowning or being trapped is not real. It's only your brain trying to convince you that you are in danger. There are ways to overcome it. I can help you, but you won't be cured overnight."

"When it's happening, I'm not sure I can think that it's not real, because it feels so real when it happens."

"Oh, it won't be easy. And it will take time. Remember, fear was put into us to protect us from real danger. But when it's irrational fear, it's not a protection, it's unfounded fear."

Corey wasn't sure how his brain worked, but Mrs. Chudzik's explanation made him feel hopeful. "Thank you, Mrs. Chudzik. I think I understand, but I don't know if I can help my family if I can't go down into the mine."

"We can work on this together, and eventually you'll be able to go down into the mine. But why do you need to work in the mine?"

"Well, now I'm thinking I'll become a breaker boy instead. I wouldn't have to go underground."

Mrs. Chudzik seemed thoughtful. "I've never believed that children should be put to work. It's just not right. Children should enjoy their childhood. They will be adults soon enough." Corey noticed Mrs. Chudzik's eyes became darker as she spoke about the boys in the mines. "The state made a law that children under twelve could no longer work in the bituminous mines, here in Pennsylvania. But there's no law that I know about boys in the anthracite mines here, where you want to work."

"Dad said I only had to be twelve to work at Mountain Crest."

"The government has no child labor laws. When they try to make a law, the states won't ratify it. Unless a law is ratified by the state, it's not a law," Mrs. Chudzik explained.

Corey didn't understand any of this. The boys worked in the mines—and that was it. No questions were ever asked.

"The mine bosses leave birth dates empty on the forms for the fathers to fill in, or sometimes it's all filled out by the mine bosses. You just watch and see if your father fills in the date of your birth. If not, the company has already put in the date they want it to be. The mines are happy the way things are. It's cheaper to hire children—they don't have to pay as much for child labor."

"You mean some fathers lie about their sons' ages?"

"Apparently so. Either that or the mine boss lies." Mrs. Chudzik put her hands in the air. "Well, that's enough talk from me. I don't deal with any of them. I just stay here in my house and mind my own business."

"My family needs money," Corey persisted. "Dad says we have bills to pay, and it's up to me as the oldest son to help out. But I don't think he'd ever lie about my age."

"Does your mother want you to work in the mines?"

"Mom's afraid I'll get hurt," Corey admitted. "She remembers a breaker boy who got caught in the machinery and squashed to death. Everyone in town remembers that day."

"Oh, yes. They brought him here. There was nothing we could do." She looked away sadly. "There are far more mine accidents with boys than with older miners. You'll need to be careful for everyone's sake, Corey, once you start at the mine."

Mrs. Chudzik took a breath and then went to the stove, where a kettle was simmering. "Now, back to your phobia, Corey. I think once a week you should come and let me know how you're doing, and we'll rehearse the things you need to do to get those dreams under control. I learned from a great teacher, but her methods were not recognized—even though they helped many people with anxiety hysteria." She poured boiling water and tea into a teapot. "Is there anything else you are afraid of?"

"No . . . well, yes." Corey remembered the bill from the company store. "I visited the company store the other day and bought some gifts for my family—for a surprise."

Mrs. Chudzik nodded. "Go on, go on."

"They put it on my account."

"Your account?" Mrs. Chudzik turned with a startled look. "They gave you an account?"

Corey nodded. "I told them I was working at the mine." He hurried to explain. "It wasn't really a *lie*. I knew I'd be working soon."

Mrs. Chudzik poured the tea into large, colorful cups. "I see. So, how much do you owe?"

Corey pulled out the bill from his pocket and handed it to her. "It's only a few dollars, but I don't have a few dollars. And neither do Mom and Dad. They were so mad at me. They weren't even happy with the gifts. Mom said she could have bought enough food for a week with that money."

"Oh, so your folks were angry."

"Dad thought I either stole the gifts or I stole money to buy the gifts." Corey looked down at his hands. He hadn't planned to share that piece of information.

Mrs. Chudzik looked the bill over and then asked, "So how do you plan to pay for this?"

"I was planning to pay for it when I started work at the mine."

"If you don't pay this off quickly, they will add interest," Mrs. Chudzik pointed out.

"I never thought about interest at the time."

"You didn't think about much, did you, when you opened that account?"

"No, I didn't," Corey admitted. He hoped Mrs. Chudzik didn't think he was stupid.

"You're not working, so where will you get the money?"

"I don't know. I don't have any money."

Mrs. Chudzik went to the kitchen counter, opened a cookie jar, and put a dish of cookies on the table. Then she looked at Corey. "I'll give you the money."

Corey gulped. "Oh, I would never ask you to do that, Mrs. Chudzik."

"You didn't ask me. But you don't get it for free. I have a requirement. I'll expect you to work for me this spring. There's quite of bit of yard work here, and I could use help."

Corey jumped up with relief. He wanted to hug Mrs. Chudzik but remembered how she'd stiffened up when he'd hugged her before. "I'll do anything you ask, Mrs. Chudzik. I'll clean up your yard, walk the dog, plant flowers. I'll be happy to do it! Thank you so much."

"Tomorrow you can pay your company store bill." She went into another room and came back with her purse. "Here you are—just in case they charge interest." She handed Corey a five-dollar bill. "Otherwise, bring me the change."

"Oh, I will, I will." Corey could hardly speak, he was so grateful.

He turned the money over in his hand. This was a *real United States bill*—not the money that Dad got in his pay envelope.

"What's the matter?" Mrs. Chudzik asked. "Haven't you ever seen a five-dollar bill before?"

"No. Dad gets paid with Mountain Crest money."

"Well, of course," Mrs. Chudzik said. "So they are still printing out their own scrip and cheating their workers in yet another way."

"Will the company store take this bill?" Corey asked.

"They will be very happy to be paid with legal tender. Just make sure your change is in real money, not scrip."

Corey nodded and put the five-dollar bill in his leather purse.

"Now, let's work on your phobia. We'll start slowly." She sat at the table again and leaned toward him. "For now, try this when you go near a mine. Stand at the entrance. That's as far as you need to go. Do not go any farther. All the while, keep thinking, or saying out loud, 'I am safe. I'm not afraid. I am only standing at the door. I don't need to be afraid or run away. Nothing is happening to hurt me.' Take your time and breathe deeply. Pay attention to how safe you are. Notice that. And don't rush. Go easy and take your time. This is your first lesson."

Corey listened intently, trying to remember every word.

"Now, this is important. *You must believe what you are telling yourself. Don't just say words—believe them.* And don't project anything more in your mind. Eventually, each time you go near a mine or into a mine, or an enclosed place, you'll find that you can go farther, but only if you choose. Just that little start will be the beginning of getting well." She pushed the plate over to him. "I'd appreciate it if you don't tell anyone about your visits here. I don't want people bothering me or running to me for help or knowing my business. I prefer to stay away from people." She looked away. "Now have a cookie."

Corey sat, took a deep breath, and felt the stress and tension leave him. He bit into a cookie. Mrs. Chudzik would help him overcome his sickness and help him pay off the company store. She had also invited him back in a week to tell her his progress.

Scary Mrs. Chudzik had calmly listened to his worries and in just a few minutes taken away all his concerns.

Whoever would believe it?

11

Abby Disappears

The next day, Corey slept until late morning. He never heard Dad getting up for work or his brothers leaving for school.

Corey decided he would go to the company store and pay off his debt. After dressing, he stuffed his leather purse and the copy of his bill into his pocket and went downstairs.

"Where are you going?" Mom asked.

"To look for work again." He ate the bologna sandwich and gulped down the milk she set before him on the table.

Mom took his hand. "I wish you didn't have to go to work, Corey."

Corey noticed Mom had slumped on a chair, and she had dark circles under her eyes. "Are you all right, Mom?"

"Yes. I get tired more than usual." She looked up at Corey. "I think you should know if you haven't guessed already. I am in a family way."

"Family way?" Corey had heard that expression many times.

"Yes, I'm going to have a baby."

"Another baby?" Now he understood why the family needed money. How could the family survive with four children when they didn't have enough money for three?

"You're surprised?" Mom said. "I thought you might have noticed that I've put on weight."

He had noticed but hadn't thought much about it. Besides, no one *ever* talked about such things. The families never said a word that they were expecting until the new baby arrived. Corey felt his face flush. "No."

"Well, I try to hide it from the neighbors, so don't tell anyone. People wonder how we can enlarge our family when money is so tight. Now you can see why we're worried about money, and why we're counting on you to help out." Mom's eyes filled up with tears. "I'm sorry to put any burden on you, Corey."

Corey couldn't stand to see his mother cry. At least now he understood why Dad was so insistent that he get a job at the mine.

"Everything will be all right, Mom," he assured her. "I'll get a job and you won't have to work so hard around here."

"Thank you, Corey."

✢ ✢ ✢

Later, as he started down the street, Mrs. Sullivan called to him from her porch. "Corey! Are you going near the company store?"

"Yes, I am," he answered as he came closer.

"Good!" She waved an envelope at him. "Would you drop this off at the store, please? My kids are sick and the visiting doctor from Scranton will be in our area today."

Corey took the envelope. "I'll put it in the doctor's box at the store," Corey said. "I hope everyone feels better."

"Maybe he'll leave a prescription for me. Or if he feels it's necessary, he'll come to our house. But we can't afford a doctor's visit." She shook her head. "Always something, when you have kids."

As he trudged down the road, Corey mimicked Mrs. Sullivan's words. "'Always something, when you have kids.'"

Almost every month, before Dad's pay envelope is ready, we go hungry and just eat beans and oatmeal. Too bad we don't have a cow or chickens, like the Sullivans. At least they have milk every day, and real butter. Mrs. Sullivan sells eggs to the neighbors too.

That's what we need to do. Maybe Mrs. Sullivan would sell us some chickens. Maybe . . .

He stopped walking and his shoulders slumped. *That's stupid. How could we get a cow or chickens? We have no money to buy them or to feed them.*

The bell on the door tinkled as Corey stepped into the company store. He dropped Mrs. Sullivan's envelope into the doctor's box, which sat on the top of a counter.

The shopkeeper came out from a back room and stood with his arms on his chest. "So, what are you lookin' to buy?"

"Nothing," Corey answered. "I'm here to pay up." Corey pulled out his coin purse and handed the salesman the bill, plus the five dollars Mrs. Chudzik had given him. "You owe me change. U.S. Treasury money, please."

The shopkeeper looked at the bill, went to the cash register, then counted out the change into Corey's hands.

"Don't forget my receipt," Corey said.

"Another week and I'd be adding interest," the man said as he scribbled on a slip of paper and handed it to Corey. "Look around and see if there's anything you need."

"Oh, no. I'm not buying anything today." He turned on his heel and left the store. If he stayed longer, he was sure to find something he wanted but didn't need.

Outside, he saw Anthony walking home from school with Abby. "Hi, Corey," Anthony called when he saw him. "Are you still lookin' for work? I heard last night that there are openings for breaker boys now."

"For breaker boys?" Corey ran to catch up with Anthony. "Now?"

"Yep, now. Mr. McBride has already signed me up. I start in two weeks, once I finish my tests at school. Then I'm done with school. Yippee. See if you can get the job, Corey. We won't get paid as much as the kids that work underground, but still, that would work for you, wouldn't it? I mean . . ." Anthony stopped and looked over at Abby as if realizing she might not know about Corey's sickness. "It would be great if you worked there too. We could join the baseball team. . . ."

"I thought you wanted to be a mule driver," Corey said.

"I can't wait until the new mules arrive. I need work now."

"I'll talk to Dad tonight about working in the breaker," Corey said. Then, turning to Abby, he asked, "What's up, Abby? Are the boys still pestering you?"

"No. I gave Billy a bloody nose when I swung my pocketbook and hit him in the face," she answered. "He ran home crying."

Corey and Anthony burst out laughing.

"You must have hit him pretty hard," Anthony said.

"I did. Maybe he'll stop bothering me now."

They had come to the corner where the road turned off to Corey's house, but Corey decided to bring Mrs. Chudzik her change. "I'm looking for work, so I thought I'd head over your way."

"There are only private homes on my street," Abby said. "But maybe someone needs yard work done."

"It's kind of early in the year for working outside," Anthony said as they approached the mining village where he lived.

"See you soon, Anthony," Corey said as his friend turned away.

"See ya soon at the breaker, Corey," Anthony said.

"Bye, Anthony," Abby called.

Shortly, Abby and Corey reached the boulder that

marked Abby's path. They stomped over old patches of snow, where early weeds were beginning to thrust themselves up between the rocks, until they reached the trail. After that, the path was better—and the trees looked newer—as if they had been chopped down at an earlier time, and the seedlings had become new trees. Funny Corey hadn't noticed this before.

He stopped to look at the huge cliff face near the top of the hill. Corey could see a massive black hole almost hidden by the dense vegetation and trees.

Where did *that* come from?" Corey asked, pointing to the cliff. "Is that an old mine? I never noticed it before."

Abby followed his gaze. "Yes, it was a mine, but it never amounted to much. Papa says the ground around here is full of hidden tunnels and old shafts. I've often wondered how blasting for new veins of coal doesn't open up some of the abandoned mines." Abby paused and motioned Corey to follow her. "Come up the hill with me. I'll show you the beautiful view at the peak of the hill, where Papa and I took a walk last week."

Corey followed her up the steep path to the top of the hill. Then they both stood, looking down at the Susquehanna River, flowing rapidly like quicksilver through the valley.

"The river is very high," Corey noticed.

"From all the snow on the mountains this year," Abby said. She pointed to the south. "See how close the Mountain Crest mine is?"

Corey could see the breaker with its black arm reaching

down greedily, as if to snatch the black diamonds—as the anthracite coal was called—still inside the earth.

"It seems about a mile away from up here, yet we walked at least three miles to get here." Corey crossed his arms. "Everything sure looks different up here on top of the mountain."

"I suppose someone in a flying machine would see things differently. It must be amazing to fly through the clouds—far above the earth—and see what the world looks like from up there," Abby said dreamily. She trotted over the rocks, pretending to be a bird. "I would love to fly more than anything." She stretched out her arms and turned around and around. "Let's go over there," she said, pointing to a level, grassy place below.

She leaped across the rocks like a butterfly, but then, with a swish and a scream—Abby disappeared!

12
Hanging On

A bby," Corey yelled as he ran toward the level spot where Abby had last stood. "Where are you?" A gaping black hole in the ground must have been covered by grass and soil on the surface.

"Help me, Corey, help me!" Abby's frantic calls came from inside the hole.

As Corey crept closer, he realized Abby had fallen into an old pipe.

Corey lay on the ground and inched his way to the edge of the opening. Looking down into the darkness, he called, "Are you hurt, Abby?" He could see her looking up, her face pale, her eyes wide with terror. Her hands were stretched up over her head, and her bloody fingers clutched the sharp edges of the pipe.

"No! My legs are spread out and my feet and my jacket are holding me. If I move, I'll fall. Help me, please, Corey."

If she could grasp his hand, he'd pull her up. But what if her hands slipped—or he didn't have the strength? She'd fall! He'd heard some of these holes could be a thousand feet deep.

He looked away. Something about the black hole and the darkness and . . . His breathing was coming in gulps. "Breathe deeply," Mrs. Chudzik had told him. "Pay attention to how safe you are."

I'm not in danger. But Abby is! I have to help her.

"Abby, what can I do?" he asked, looking down at his friend again. The smell of rust and decay wafted up the pipe. Abby was drowning . . . no . . . Abby was *trapped*, like he had been when he had fallen into the pond.

"Get something for me to hang on to—something that won't let me fall," she called. "Hurry."

He looked around the top of the cliff and found a branch that must have fallen in a snowstorm. It was big and heavy, and little twigs were breaking through like spikes. Abby couldn't hold on to this with her small hands. He tossed it aside.

"Corey, I need you to help me," Abby called again, her voice echoing from inside the pipe. "If I fall, I could die. Find something—do something!"

Corey recognized the cold darkness coiling around him like a serpent—the fear closing in—the need to breathe, to break his way out, to fight for his life. But wait.

That was the panic that overcame him in a dream or in the tunnels of the mine. Not here. Why now? He didn't understand, but he couldn't stop the panic.

He moved to the pipe again, his eyes glued to the black hole. "I . . . can't find anything that would work. I don't know what to do."

"What's wrong? You sound far away."

"I'm here . . . near the hole."

"Corey! What's wrong?" Abby called. Her voice broke. "I need you to help me."

Corey moved away from the hole and the pipe that sank far into the mountain, where the knockers dwelled. He knew the horrors in the mines—the hard stone walls and roofs, the cave-ins with no way out. Thousands of miners had died in those tunnels, and their bodies were never recovered. Sweat poured from his forehead and mixed with the tears that now flowed down his cheeks.

"Corey! Are you there?"

"I . . . I'm here, but something is happening . . . to me."

"Corey! Nothing is happening to you. *I'm the one who needs help.*"

Corey looked up at the blue sky above. He wasn't in the hole, but fear had imprisoned him as if he were the one trapped in the pipe.

What were the words Mrs. Chudzik had told him to recite? He couldn't remember.

"Corey, Corey, where are you?" Abby was sobbing.

He couldn't answer. He couldn't help Abby. He couldn't

climb into the pipe to save her—he couldn't even look *down into that pipe.*

As the world swirled around him, Corey backed away from the hole to a nearby tree. He wrapped his trembling arms around it, closed his eyes, and held on for dear life.

13
Amazing Abby

Time seemed endless while Corey clung to the tree and blocked out the world. When he finally opened his eyes, the sun was low and the shadows were deep.

Was Abby still in the pipe, or had she fallen to the bottom? Could she have held on all this time? "Abby!" Where was she now? He let go of the comforting tree, got onto his knees, and crawled toward the gaping hole.

"Abby, are . . . are you there?"

"I'm over here."

Corey spun around to see Abby hunched up on a rock.

"Are you all right? How did you get out?"

"I was able to push myself up little by little until I got to the top and climbed onto the grass again."

"I wanted to help you. . . ." He stopped. There was

nothing he could say. He was a coward and Abby knew it.

"It took a long time, and I slipped back a few times, but I made it by myself." Abby stretched out her hands for him to see. Her fingers were raw with scrapes and cuts, and her nails were broken.

"Oh, Abby, your poor hands." He could hardly speak. "I'm sorry I couldn't do anything, but when I looked down into the pipe and saw you hanging in there, I froze."

Abby didn't speak for a while. When she got to her feet, she winced as she brushed off her clothes. "Once I got out, I wanted to run and leave you here by yourself." She shook her head and sighed. "But I also remembered all the times you stuck up for me when the boys were mean. I knew that you would have helped me if you could. I realized you are sick, Corey. I never saw anyone as sick as you. And the way you hugged that tree . . . well, I don't understand what was happening to you, but I couldn't leave until I knew you were all right."

Corey thought of Abby down there alone and frightened and how he had failed her, yet here she was telling him that she understood that he couldn't help her or himself.

"Let's get out of here," he said. "But first I'll roll this boulder over the hole so no one else can fall in."

Corey and Abby walked silently until they came to the trail. Then she said, "Papa should be home from work, and I think he'll want to talk with you when he hears what happened up there."

Corey dreaded facing Mr. Russell. There was nothing

he could say in his own defense. The pain he was feeling, at his failure to help her, was even worse than the terror.

He walked with her to the hill behind Mrs. Chudzik's and the Russells' houses. Then he stopped. "I . . . can't talk to your father right now. I've got to see Mrs. Chudzik. That's where I was going when I met you earlier. Then I've got to get home. Mom will be worried to death, and she . . . she's not well."

"Oh, I see," Abby said, walking away.

"Good-bye, Abby. I . . . I'm glad you're okay . . . except for your hands . . . ," he stammered. "You're right, Abby. I am sick."

He ran toward the big gray house. He had to talk with Mrs. Chudzik right away.

14

Sympathetic Character

Hovi must have seen Corey through the window, because he barked as Corey ran across the grass from Abby's house.

He climbed the steps to the porch, and before he could pull the handle on the ugly knocker, Mrs. Chudzik opened the door a crack and peered out. "Who's there?"

"It's me, Corey."

She opened the door wide and waved Corey inside and down the hall to the kitchen. Mrs. Chudzik didn't look as scary today. She was dressed in a long blue skirt, a white blouse, and a blue sweater that matched the skirt. She looked quite nice, with her silvery hair swept up in a bun. Under the electric light over the table, he noticed for the first time that her eyes were blue and they didn't bulge as they did from behind her driving goggles.

"So, where were you that you're running and out of breath?" she asked after they sat down at the oak table.

Corey told her how Abby had fallen into the pipe on the cliff and how he'd had one of his spells and couldn't do anything to help. "I failed her."

She listened without a comment until he was finished. Then she said, "I find it interesting that *Abby's* fall set off *your* phobia. This tells me you are a sympathetic character and explains why you reacted so powerfully to Abby's predicament."

"Sympathetic character?"

"Someone who is sensitive to another person's pain. When your friend Abby was in danger, you reacted as if it were happening to you."

She leaned toward Corey and her blue eyes darkened. "Listen to me. No matter what happened up there on the cliff, don't you believe for one minute that you are a failure or a coward. It is not true." She sat back. "You are a sensitive young man who cares deeply about others and who will do something remarkable and heroic one day."

Corey looked down at the checkered tablecloth. *How could she think such good things about me when everything I do proves the opposite?* Yet once again, Mrs. Chudzik made him feel better. She understood. *She is the sympathetic character*, he realized.

"What you need right now is a good cup of tea." She got

up and put tea in the pot and then poured steaming water from the kettle on it. "My husband and I never knew there were open shafts on that property. It's fortunate that no one has had an accident before." She shook her head. "I must have everything sealed up right away, before someone gets killed."

"Is there a map that shows the mine chutes and shafts?"

"The map was very old. It only shows my property *before* that mine started working. I already gave it to Mr. Russell. He is looking for more information or maps to bring the records up to date. I'm sure he'll be even more concerned now that Abby fell into that vent." She poured the tea into cups.

"I was heading this way to bring you the change from the five dollars you loaned me, when I ran into Abby." Corey emptied the leather change purse into his palm and handed her the money. "Thank you so much for helping me, Mrs. Chudzik." When she didn't answer, Corey continued, "I paid off my debt this afternoon, and now I don't owe anyone—except, of course, for the work I owe you."

She placed a dish of cookies on the table and sat down again. "I knew you might be coming by, so I made cookies." She took a sip of tea. "Do your folks believe now that you did not steal the money?"

"I hope so. They've promised not to speak of it again."

"They know you wouldn't bring shame to the family by stealing. Anyone can see that." Mrs. Chudzik leaned across the table and said intently, "That day at the pond, I didn't think you'd make it, but you fought hard and you lived. There's a reason you survived that you'll understand some-day." She sipped her tea again.

It was hard to understand what Mrs. Chudzik meant after he'd confessed to her that he couldn't help Abby. "The cookies are good," he said, trying to change the subject. "My Polish grandma used to make these same cookies." He sipped his tea. "Dad's family is Polish, and my mother's side of the family was from Wales."

"Wales was one of the first places to find anthracite coal," she told him. "So mining goes far back on both sides of your family."

"My nana—my mother's mother—used to tell me Welsh stories about the mines."

"Aha—like the ones about the knockers?"

"She called them Coblynau. That's the Gaelic word for 'knockers,'" he explained. "They were the elves that lived in the mines and—"

"And knocked to warn that the mines were about to collapse. We have similar stories in Poland."

Corey thought for a moment. "But if the knockers warned the miners, they would have been good, wouldn't they? I always thought the knockers were wicked. The Coblynau would steal the miners' tools and lunches . . . and play all sorts of tricks on them."

"If they are good or bad depends on the story," Mrs. Chudzik said.

"I miss Nana and Gram," Corey said. "I have no grand-mothers now."

Mrs. Chudzik nodded. "Did they tell you the tales about hellhounds?"

This is getting strange. Does Mrs. Chudzik know that people think Hovi is a hellhound? "Um, yes. My grandpa from Wales teased me with spooky stories of the devil dogs with their bloody fangs." He glanced down at Hovi, who slept on the floor next to his chair.

"Do phobias go away? Or will I have it all my life?" he asked, suddenly coming back to the subject he dreaded. "I've been wondering . . . and almost afraid to ask."

"Once you convince yourself that you are not in danger, it may go away, or at least, not be as severe. As I told you, though, recovery will take time. Remember, it's only been one day since we talked, and you haven't had time to practice."

"Will I have panic attacks all my life?" Corey asked again.

"I don't know. You may want to stay away from the mines or swimming or whatever might precipitate the phobia. But you may never know when one might come upon you. However, there are ways to avoid them or diminish them."

"I tried to recite the words you told me, but when I was with Abby today, I couldn't even think." He frowned, trying to recall the words. "'I am safe. I'm not afraid. I don't need to be afraid or run away. Nothing is happening to hurt me.'" His shoulders slumped. "A lot of good it does me now."

"Try not to dwell on what happened today," Mrs. Chudzik said.

"Did you ever know someone else who had them like I do? The seizures . . . or whatever you call them?"

She nodded but didn't answer. Instead she looked at the clock. "It's suppertime. I should get you home right away."

15

Mrs. Chudzik Speaks Up

It was suppertime when they arrived in Mrs. Chudzik's car. Corey had told Mom he was going to look for work today. So perhaps she wasn't upset and thought he had found work and just hadn't come home yet.

"Please come in, Mrs. Chudzik," Corey begged. "It will help if you're there to explain what happened today." He was certain that his parents would not scream at him with Mrs. Chudzik there.

With a sigh, Mrs. Chudzik turned off the car and headed to the house with Corey. "Stay!" she ordered Hovi, who sat back obediently, looking miffed.

Corey opened the front door and called out, "Mom? Dad? I'm home."

Mom appeared from the kitchen. Seeing Mrs. Chudzik,

she looked surprised, and then concerned. "Why, Mrs. Chudzik, has Corey been at your house all this time?"

"Not exactly. There was an incident—up on the hill near my house. Abby Russell fell into a pipe up there and Corey was with her at the time. He wasn't hurt," Mrs. Chudzik explained. "Abby is fine too."

Dad came in from the kitchen and stood by the door with a perplexed look. "What now?"

Corey moved closer to Mrs. Chudzik. "Abby Russell fell into a mine shaft. But everything is all right, Dad."

Mom asked, "How did she get out?"

"She was able to pull herself out," Mrs. Chudzik answered.

"Seems like wherever Corey goes, there's trouble," Dad muttered.

"Corey had nothing to do with her fall," Mrs. Chudzik answered quickly. "No one knew there was a pipe there— hidden from sight. She stepped on the ground, and down she went."

Mom gasped. "Good heavens. How far down did she fall?"

"Not far," Corey answered. "Her jacket caught her and she stretched out her legs and her feet and stopped her fall. She got out by herself."

"Oh, thank God you didn't drop in there with her. You could have both been killed!" Mom exclaimed.

Dad frowned. "Those ventilation passages and abandoned mines are all over the place."

Mrs. Chudzik continued, "Mr. Russell is planning to

make a map of all the mine shafts that may be around this area. Part of that mine is on my property, I'm sorry to say."

"The ground underneath this whole area of coal country is a maze of underground tunnels," Dad said.

"When I think what might have happened if they'd both fallen down into the pipe . . . Why, we might never have found them." Mom's eyes filled with tears.

"I hope you learned a lesson," Dad said, shaking a finger at Corey. "You need to realize the seriousness of the decisions you make, like going up that cliff when you don't know what dangers are there. You've got to *stop acting like a child!*"

For a moment there was silence, and then Mrs. Chudzik spoke up in a soft voice. "But, Mr. Adamski, *Corey is a child.* He's *just beginning* to learn the dangers and the seriousness of life and how to make the right choices. Isn't it a bit early to judge him as an adult?"

Dad stood there with his mouth open, red-faced and unable to answer, when Mom spoke up.

"That's true. He's only a child—and a good child at that. We shouldn't expect so much of him."

Dad nodded, and gradually the tension waned.

Mrs. Chudzik stayed long enough for a cup of tea, and then, after promises that they would all get together for a real Polish dinner next Sunday, Corey walked her out to her car. Hovi whined as Corey patted him. Mom and Dad waved good-bye and called thank you from the front porch.

After she had left, Dad was curious. "Corey, why is it

when you are in trouble, you end up at Mrs. Chudzik's front door?"

"I don't know, Dad. I guess it's because her house happens to be the closest at the time."

"It is strange, isn't it?" Mom added.

"She did tell me that in China if someone saves your life, that person becomes responsible for your life forever," Corey admitted.

"Oh, I hope Mrs. Chudzik doesn't feel she must be responsible for you forever," Mom said.

Dad snorted as he went inside. "It's fine with me. We need all the help we can get with Corey."

16
Inspecting the Ventilation Shaft

When Corey woke up the next morning, he went down to the kitchen, where Mom was cleaning up the breakfast dishes. Dad had gone to work, and Jack and Sammy had already left for school.

"How are you feeling?" Mom asked him.

"I'm just fine."

She took the broom and began her morning sweep of the entire house: the doors, the porch, the walk—everything. The coal dust was in the very air around mine country. Mom did the wash two or three times a week and hung it out on the clothesline. But by the time she brought it in, later in the afternoon, it was already overlaid with coal dust.

"I don't suppose we'll ever get away from the coal

and the dust," she said. "This will be our lives and our deaths, too. It's in our lungs. Both your grandfathers died from black lung disease. The only way we'll get away from the dirt is to die, and then they bury us in it." Mom slammed the broom against the wall with an angry whack.

Corey hated to see his mother so unhappy. "Mom, I'm going to be a breaker boy real soon. Things will be better then, you'll see." Corey pulled on his jacket and started out the door.

"Where are you going?"

"I'm going to see how Abby is today."

"Well, go ahead, but don't go up on that cliff again. Keep in mind that there's danger right under your feet once you go off the beaten track."

"Mom, don't worry so much."

Corey headed to Abby's house. He wanted to apologize to Mr. Russell, that he didn't do something to help Abby. He hoped he could explain his phobia, as he certainly didn't want the Russells to think he was a coward. He wished they would forgive him—or that maybe Mrs. Chudzik would speak for him to Abby's family, like she had with Dad. He hoped and prayed that his own father wouldn't find out the truth—that Corey, his oldest son, hadn't done a single thing to help Abby.

At Abby's house, Mr. and Mrs. Russell gave him a warm welcome and shook his hand.

"You just missed Abby. She left for school a half hour ago," Mrs. Russell said. "Thank you, Corey, for staying with our Abby and reassuring her the way you did."

Didn't they know how he'd failed? Maybe Abby never told them.

Corey was bewildered. Should he just let them go on thinking whatever it was they believed? Or should he confess how he froze with fear and clung to that stupid tree? He decided he'd wait until he talked with Abby again. He was about to leave when the doorbell rang.

"It's your father," Mr. Russell said, ushering Dad into the kitchen. "He wants to see where the accident occurred yesterday. He's coming with me to put up the 'danger' sign and see what the pipe is and where it goes. Why don't you come with us, Corey? You can lead us directly to the pipe."

Corey looked to see what Dad might be thinking. "Sure. I can do that," he answered.

"Fine with me," Dad said.

Mr. Russell put the DANGER sign he'd made into a valise and tucked it under his arm, and the three of them headed toward the old mine.

When Dad noticed the cavernous opening in the wall of the cliff, he asked, "How long ago was that a working mine?"

"Maybe fifty years ago or more," Mr. Russell answered. "That opening you see only goes in a little way because of a cave-in that blocked off the entrance. No one's been able to get in there since—unless there's another entrance that we don't know about. There could be poisonous gas in there or treacherous holes . . . who knows? There are no old maps of the mine itself." He held up a yellowed roll of paper. "This is the oldest one. The deed to Mrs. Chudzik's property doesn't show the mine. I need to get a crew in here to survey the whole area, but I don't know if the powers that be will want to spend the money."

Dad rolled his eyes. "Money ranks number one among the mine barons. Never mind danger or loss of the miners' limbs or lives. Why, there have been accidents when a boy gets caught in the machinery and the breaker stops. The bosses insist that the breaker should keep running until the end of the day—despite who might be dead in the machinery."

"I heard that happened only once," Corey muttered with a warning look at his father. Did Dad forget that Mr. Russell was an engineer for the company and not a common miner? He hoped Dad would be more careful of what he was saying to someone as prominent as Mr. Russell.

The men and Corey headed into the mine. Dad glanced at his son with a questioning look, as if to say, *Are you all right? Shouldn't you stay out of here?*

Corey nodded and whispered, "I'm okay."

The cavity leading into the mine was large and open, and Corey remembered what Mrs. Chudzik had suggested—to breathe deeply and stay close to the opening, keeping in mind that he didn't have to go in there and everything was all right. So Corey stood close to the entrance and silently repeated those words over and over.

Corey watched in awe as Mr. Russell brought out a small, portable battery-powered electric lamp and turned it on. Corey had never seen one but had heard of this new invention that some people called a flashlight. How amazing that without a cord or wire, the flashlight could be carried around in a man's satchel to be used anywhere. Mr. Russell was near the back of the cavern, and the light revealed another black crevice that burrowed even deeper into the wall of the cliff. How deep into the mountain did it go before the rubble from the cave-in blocked the way?

Mr. Russell came back and took out his notebook, scribbled some information in it, and then summoned Dad and Corey to leave. "Let's go up the cliff now. I'll be coming back here later," he said. He handed Corey a piece of coal. "This has a nice fossil on it. I found it near the entrance. It could be a million years old. I thought you might like to have it."

Corey held the coal in his hand, amazed at the perfect impression of a leaf, with all its little veins. *A million years ago*, Corey thought. It was as if the world had held that fossil for all that time waiting for Corey. He loved the fossil. It was another wonder, beautiful and mystifying.

"I would like to investigate just how far into the ground the mine went and if it goes below water level," Mr. Russell said.

"How do you measure it?" Corey asked.

"Good question," Mr. Russell said with a grin. "I had to go to school for four years or more to figure that one out!"

They emerged from the cavern and began their climb up the cliff to the top of the hill.

"Watch your step," Dad said. "It's almost as bad outside the mines as inside. Anyone could fall into a shaft and never be found."

"There's danger, all right, especially for boys in the mines," Mr. Russell said. "Some of those kids are only nine or ten years old and could slip down into a hole easily and be lost. Their folks are so eager to get them to work to help out with the family expenses, they lie about their ages."

"If the miners got the pay that they should, they wouldn't have to send their boys to work," Dad retorted.

"I thought the miners were satisfied with the pay since they joined the union and had the big strike a few years ago."

"Things are better, but there's a long way to go," Dad answered.

"Miners need to be careful how they spend their money. I see many of them on paydays, drinking their money away in the saloons."

Corey could see where this conversation was heading. "We're almost to the top. Watch out for hidden pipes," he said in a loud voice, hoping his father would get the message.

But Dad couldn't let Mr. Russell's last comment go. "You've never *seen me* in those saloons," he snapped. "And we conserve our money as best we can. Why, my wife doesn't even buy underwear for anyone. She makes it out of the old muslin the mine throws out. I'll bet your daughter never wore scratchy muslin underwear," Dad said defiantly. "My wife cans vegetables from her own garden."

"She is certainly very resourceful," Mr. Russell answered uncomfortably. "Shall we look for that pipe now? Is it nearby, Corey?"

They had reached the crest of the hill, where Abby and Corey had stood yesterday. "Look at the river," Corey said. "It's wild."

"We'd better not get more rain," Mr. Russell said. "The river is way above flood stage now. More rain and all the melting snow from upstate could cause a major disaster."

"We've had some bad floods in the past around here," Dad said.

Corey pointed to the south. "Look how close we are to the Mountain Crest mine. The breaker looks as if it could reach over here and pick us up."

"I've been to the top of the breaker but never realized I was looking at this hill right near my house," Mr. Russell said.

Corey was relieved to hear the topic of conversation change. "There's the boulder I put over the hole where Abby fell," Corey said, pointing. "It looked level and grassy, and you'd never know it was there before Abby dropped into it. Poor Abby jumped right down onto that pipe."

Mr. Russell pulled the rock away and flashed his portable light into the pipe. "It's a long way down." He stood aside and handed the flashlight to Dad, who peered down too.

"That would be a terrible fall," Dad agreed with a whistle.

Mr. Russell pulled a boulder over the opening and then taped the DANGER sign to it. Dad gathered more rocks and placed them around the edges of the hole.

"The bright red letters stand out as a warning, but more needs to be done to seal this up permanently." Mr. Russell turned to Corey. "Corey, we are so thankful that you were with Abby when she fell. But you could have fallen in too, and we might never have known. . . ." He closed his eyes and shook his head, as if blotting out the frightful image from his mind.

Corey was uncomfortable taking credit for something he never did and was about to blurt out what had really happened, when Mr. Russell spoke again.

"We'll need to survey this whole area and make triangulations to figure out the height of this hill. Then I'd like to go into the old mine and see how deep into the earth it goes and how far to the south. I don't know any way to get into the old mine, except through this pipe, which would be a tight squeeze. In the old days, they didn't have to have two entrances to a mine in case of emergency. Perhaps there was just one entrance."

Corey looked Mr. Russell up and down. He was tall and thin. "I think you might be able to squirm down through the pipe," he said. "Abby had on her big coat and there was still room. She had to keep her legs out to hold herself up."

Dad was gazing thoughtfully at the Mountain Crest breaker in the distance. "I wonder if we might actually be blasting that new chamber in Mountain Crest too near the chambers here."

"If you blast too close to this mine, it might cause another roof fall or release dangerous gases." Mr. Russell scribbled something into his notebook and then put it into the valise.

"I'm going to hammer this concern into the brains of the bosses up there." He winked at Dad. "I'll tell them there's a possibility of a bad accident here and that could be a huge lawsuit."

"A lawsuit? That should get their attention," Dad said with a laugh. He put out his hand to Mr. Russell. "Sorry I got carried away with my complaints. Sometimes I talk too much."

Mr. Russell shook Dad's hand. "Between both of us, maybe we'll get some help to close up these old shafts."

Dad started down the steep cliff. "I wish Corey didn't have to go to work in the mines, but I don't know what else we can do. Mining is in my blood. I guess you'd say it's a family tradition. I began in the mines when I was Corey's age."

"Who knows? Maybe it will be different for Corey," Mr. Russell said. "Thanks for coming with me. The bosses up at the mine may now pay attention to the dangers out here." Mr. Russell put his arm around Corey's shoulder. "Did Abby tell you what she heard down in the pipe while she was hanging in there?" Mr.

Russell asked as they walked down the hill.

"No," Corey answered.

"She said she heard knocking," Mr. Russell said. "She's convinced it was the knockers. Poor Abby was so frightened she could have imagined anything."

17

First Day as a Breaker Boy

Things happened fast during the next couple of days. Corey was determined to help out with the family finances. Since he was feeling better and certain he would not have to go down into the mine itself, he was ready to work at the breaker. He hoped he could get on the baseball team he'd heard so much about. He was a good player in the neighborhood games.

It was the first day of Corey's employment at the Mountain Crest colliery, and Corey was up before the sun rose. Mom had set out an old pair of black trousers, a shirt, and a cap that she had cleaned up and repaired. They wouldn't stay clean for long.

"Mrs. Balaski gave us this extra lunch pail that she had in her pantry, and I packed a meat loaf sandwich that you'll love," Mom said. "There's a slice of Aunt Millie's apple pie, and a slice of her peach pie made with her own wonderful preserves, so you're going to have a grand lunch on your first day."

"Thanks, Mom."

"I've made you a good breakfast," Mom said, pushing a plate of bacon and eggs under his nose.

"I'm just not hungry. . . ." Then, seeing Mom's crestfallen face, he added, "I'm nervous—well, excited to be going to work."

"You'll be starving by lunchtime if you don't have breakfast. . . ."

"So I'll eat everything in my lunch box, then."

"I've put in a vacuum bottle of hot coffee," Mom said. "Now that you're a working member of the family, you'll need coffee—it's what miners have every day to give them energy." She looked at Corey's hands. "They'll be sore and red when you get home."

"Can I wear gloves?" he asked.

"No, the bosses won't let you. With gloves on, you can't feel the differences in the coal."

Corey probably would never be a real miner, although he recalled Mrs. Chudzik telling him that he would get over his phobia in time—or that that he'd be better, at least. For now he would only work in the breaker—the big building with the chute that lifted the coal to the top and then dropped it down through the conveyer, where the breaker boys waited to pull out rocks, slate, and stones that didn't belong in with the anthracite coal. People around the country didn't want to pay for expensive anthracite and find rocks mixed in. Anthracite was called "black diamonds" because it was harder than bituminous coal and more valuable because it burned longer.

"You look like a breaker boy, except for one thing. You're as clean as a cat," Dad said, looking Corey up and down. "When you come home tonight, you'll be covered with coal dust like the rest of us."

"I hope no one will know I'm new. Maybe I could say I worked in another mine and just moved to this one."

"No, you don't want to lie. Besides, you know some of the boys, who will know you're new," Dad said. "They might tease you a bit. And maybe play a trick or two—like stealing your lunch. They did that to me when I worked in the breaker. Just grin and bear it and you'll be one of the boys in no time."

Corey knew some of the breaker boys who'd gone to school with him from first grade until they left to work in the breaker in third grade. A few boys he remembered were the Slavic boys. They were always a friendly group who minded their own business. Corey supposed it was because they didn't speak English and they had a different alphabet. They ended up leaving school and going to work at the breaker too.

"I hope I'll make some friends," Corey said wistfully to his dad. "And I hope I can play on the baseball team."

"They'll be lucky to have you on the team and as a friend," Dad said.

✢ ✢ ✢

The colliery was about two or three miles down the road—beyond the company store, and the town itself. Corey felt edgy as they neared the giant breaker that stood silhouetted near the top of the hill.

Dad took Corey to the superintendent and signed papers. The superintendent gave them a birth certificate, and Corey noticed his age was already penned in as twelve and eligible to work.

Dad waved good-bye, and a boy named Charlie took Corey to the washroom, where the breaker boys cleaned up and left their lunch pails. Corey found an empty cube and shoved his in there. If he concealed it well enough, the boys couldn't hide it on him, he figured.

"Stop the breaker!" Charlie called to someone who ran the conveyer. The command was repeated all the way to the top. The grinding, noisy conveyor came to a slow halt. Then Charlie yelled to another boy who stood nearby. "Hey, Frank! Come over here and show this kid how you tell the good stuff from the bad stuff."

Corey wanted to say, "I know the difference between the anthracite and the junk rocks," but decided against it. Something about Charlie and Frank—the way they swaggered as if they were in charge and knew everything—gave Corey the feeling that he should keep his mouth shut.

He followed Frank to the conveyer belt, found a seat, and let Frank show him the sharp gray slate and the plain rocks that were mixed in with or part of the shiny black coal. "Throw the bad stuff into another chute,"

Frank said. "Got it?" Corey nodded. "Then get to work!" Frank signaled someone at the top to turn the conveyor back on, and the scraping sounds started again.

So Corey began his job as a breaker boy.

At lunchtime, the conveyor stopped, and the boys all trooped into the washroom, stood in line to remove the black soot from their hands, then grabbed their lunch pails and headed for the yard outside. The fresh air "cleaned the black soot from your lungs," the miners had been told. Black lung disease was never cured by fresh air, Corey knew. Even the air around the coal mines was full of coal dust.

As Corey cleaned the black dust from his hands, he gulped in pain. The cold water smarted, and he could now see the red welts and the cuts from the sharp rocks. He couldn't let the other boys see how much he was hurting. He swaggered a little himself, and acted like he was fine, but his fingers were bleeding and sore. If he could just find his cube, he'd get his lunch and get outside.

The cubicles all looked alike, and now Corey wasn't sure which one he'd used to hold his lunch. He stood around waiting, hoping that his would be the one left. However, by the time everyone had gone, he still couldn't find his lunch pail. And he was hungry, too.

"Lookin' for somethin', kid?" asked Frank, who waited by the door with a mocking grin.

"No," Corey answered.

Corey followed Frank outside, a bit wary and hoping he'd find someone who had seen or taken his lunch. A few kids paid no attention to him, while others stood aside and whispered to one another.

"So, where's your dinner pail?" Frank finally asked.

"I dunno. I must have lost it," Corey answered. "Have you seen it?"

"You lost your lunch?" another boy asked as he sauntered up to them. "Too bad. We found one that had a great meat loaf sandwich. It was delicious."

A couple of younger boys joined in. "It had the best pies we've had in a long time."

Corey realized the boys had played a dirty trick on him, just as Dad had warned. He hoped the boys didn't have anything else in mind. But a boy named Paddy had something more to say. "See that little fellow over there? That's Shorty." He pointed to a kid who was so small he looked about eight years old and who carried a huge oilcan. "He has something for you."

Now what? Corey wondered.

"Come over here, Shorty," Paddy yelled to the little kid.

"Shorty has the huge, important job of oiling the machinery every lunchtime. He gets an extra quarter a week for doin' this key job," Paddy explained. He took the big oilcan from Shorty and showed it to Corey. "See this? It's grease. We discovered that new guys need to be greased every day too. So they don't get too stuck on themselves."

Corey noticed that a crowd of boys had surrounded him, closing in from every direction.

"That's right," someone said. "New guys need oiling every day." The boys were laughing.

Paddy came closer. "Stand still while we give you a greasing." He pulled out the back of Corey's pants and squirted something wet and cold down his trousers.

"Hey!" he yelled. "Knock it off!" He thrashed around, punching at everyone who was near. He was able to get a good wallop at Paddy's face.

Paddy yelled and swore. "He got me. Someone else take over!"

For a second, Corey felt good. He saw Paddy's face covered with blood and knew he had made a direct hit on that rotten kid's nose. But his victory was short-lived as another kid grabbed the can from Paddy and continued squirting the smelly grease into Corey's trousers.

Corey tried to pull away, but several boys held on to him until his pants were completely full of the thick, greasy oil and it was trickling down his legs. Then, as swift and noisy as a flock of crows, the breaker boys disappeared to the other side of the field, leaving Corey standing alone, legs apart and very well greased.

18
Sticky Business

Now what do I do? Corey wondered. He was sticky, hot, and hungry, and his fingers and hands were brutally sore from working all morning at the breaker.

Dad warned me the kids might steal my lunch or play little tricks, but no one told me that the other boys would be just plain rotten and mean—that they'd pour grease down my pants. And they made fun of me—that was the worst part.

The colliery whistle pierced the air, calling the boys back to work as the lunch hour ended.

No way would Corey go back—not with all the grease dripping down and his clothes sticking. Instead, he watched as the boys stopped their ball game and gathered into lines that disappeared into the great black dragonlike breaker.

Once the boys were gone, Corey took off across the field and onto the path that led home. The thick, sticky grease in his trousers clung to his body and slipped down his legs and out through the bottom of his pants, leaving a trail of oily slime on the ground as he ran.

Finally, gasping and sweating, hurting and hungry, he saw the line of houses where he lived. If he could just soak in the big tin tub and get all this sludge off . . . Mom would have some salve for his poor hands.

He thought about the neighborhood kids who'd known he was going to work. They'd never let him live it down. He actually wished he had stayed in school and never left Miss O'Shea's class. School wasn't as bad as the breaker and the guys who worked there.

As he ran up the steps to the porch, his breath came in gasps that turned into moans. "Mom? Mom!" No one answered. The door was locked, and he sank to the floor of the porch and banged his fists, and then cried out as his hands began bleeding. "Mom!"

Corey got up and ran to the backyard to the clothesline, where Mom set the laundry out two or three times a week. The clothes swung in the wind, like dancing paper dolls.

If he took some clean clothes off the line, he could go to someone's house and clean up. But where? Mrs. Balaski next door was nice, but she was usually helping out her elderly mom every day. The more neighbors who knew what happened, the more people would laugh and talk about him and how he couldn't take being a breaker boy.

He sat on the back steps and thought. Aunt Millie! Sure, that's where he'd go—even though it would be a long walk to the other side of Wilkes-Barre, where she lived. Aunt Millie was usually home this time of day, and she'd help him.

He went to the clothesline, pulled off clean clothes and underwear, piled it all into a towel, and pinned it together with several clothespins. After gathering the bundle into his arms, he started the trek across town.

He had walked a few miles, mostly uphill, and he was hungry, thirsty, and miserable. His clothes stuck to him with the sticky grease, and his hands were bleeding. He would turn around and go home, except he'd have to face Dad. What would Dad think if he lost his job on his first day as a breaker boy because he didn't return after lunch? Couldn't Corey take a little horseplay from the other boys? What would everyone think of him for walking away from the breaker and his new job?

He was about to turn around, head home, and face the music, when he saw a red car coming up the road toward him. The driver honked the musical horn, and the dog in the front passenger seat barked. It was Mrs. Chudzik and Hovi!

"Where are you going?" Mrs. Chudzik shouted from her chariot.

"To my aunt Millie's, across the bridge."

"Get in," she called to him. "Show me the way and I'll take you there."

"It's out of your way," Corey protested—but not convincingly. He was never so glad to see anyone.

"Backseat, Hovi!" she ordered the dog. She reached over and opened the passenger door.

Corey climbed in the car and sat on the edge of the luxurious leather seat, while Mrs. Chudzik turned the car around.

"Why are you walking way over there this time of day?" Eyeing the big bundle he carried, she asked, "Are you running away from home?"

"Um, n-no . . . ," he stammered. "I'm going to Aunt Millie's to take a bath."

"Can't you take a bath at your own house?"

So Corey told his story—how he started work as a breaker boy, what the boys did to him, and how his house was locked, so he decided to go to Aunt Millie for help.

"Let me get this right. You ran away from work because the boys put the grease down your pants and stole your lunch?" Mrs. Chudzik asked.

Corey's story sounded lame when she told it—as if he was a sissy and ran away. "And because my hands are all bleeding and sore," he said, adding a little more misery to the tale. He held out his hands to Mrs. Chudzik. "See?"

Mrs. Chudzik looked down at his hands through her thick goggles. "Well, I have some salve that will fix up those cuts. Why don't you come over to my house and have your bath there, and then I'll take you back to the breaker."

"I don't want to go back to the breaker after what happened."

"Well, we'll see," Mrs. Chudzik said as she turned her chariot around again.

19
The Skeleton

Later, at Mrs. Chudzik's house, Corey waited in the kitchen while Mrs. Chudzik disappeared somewhere. Meanwhile, Hovi crept closer and stretched out on the floor in front of Corey, his tail still wagging.

"Good boy, Hovi." The dog turned over onto his back, four legs in the air. Corey reached down and gingerly scratched the dog's soft belly with his sore fingers.

Corey heard water running as Mrs. Chudzik came into the kitchen. "Here's what we'll do. You can take a hot bath and get the grease off you. Then get into your clean clothes and I'll take you back." She motioned for Corey to follow her, and he and Hovi trailed her into a room that looked like an office.

Over by the window, sickly white against the darkness

of the room, with a miner's hat and light perched upon its head, was a grinning skeleton—and it was glaring straight at him! Corey stopped dead in his tracks.

"Oh, that's my husband's skeleton," Mrs. Chudzik explained.

Corey's weak knees just about gave out on him. Mrs. Chudzik kept Dr. Chudzik's skeleton right here in her house? "You . . . mean that is . . . was . . . Dr. Chudzik?"

"No! That is not my husband. Dr. Chudzik bought that skeleton for his medical practice. Paid a lot for it too. We named him Zerak, which means 'guardian of the king' . . . the king being my husband, of course."

"Is . . . is it *real?* Is it someone's bones?"

"No one we know." She opened a door to another room. "This is the bathroom, and as you see, the tub is filling and almost ready." Steaming hot water and suds billowed in the white porcelain bathtub, filling the room with the aroma of soap and pine trees. "Take your bath, get yourself clean, and then we'll fix up your hands. Those cuts need to be cleaned and will probably sting in the water, but you can stand it, I'm sure." She was about to leave the room. Hovi stayed, looking at Mrs. Chudzik with pleading eyes. "Hovi wants to stay in here with you."

"He can stay." Corey removed his shoes. "Where did you get that name, Hovi?"

"He is a Hovawart—an ancient German breed. Let me tell you something about this dog. Hovi is gentle and obedient, but he never runs away from a challenge.

Something for you to think about." She went out of the room but left the door open.

As Corey undressed, he could see Zerak grinning at him from the office. "Mrs. Chudzik," Corey called. "Zerak is staring at me . . . and I'm stark naked."

"This *is* a doctor's office," Mrs. Chudzik reminded him. "Zerak has seen naked patients before."

"Please close the door, Mrs. Chudzik."

The door shut—as if by itself.

20
Corey's Bath

Corey sank into the warm water. *What did Mrs. Chudzik mean about running away from challenges? Did she mean that I ran from those breaker boys? Well, who wouldn't?*

Corey put his hands cautiously into the water. "Ouch!" he cried out as they stung and smarted.

Hovi sat up from his place on the rug, put his front paws on the side of the tub, and whined. The golden fur above his eyes rose in worry as he watched Corey anxiously.

"Aw, I'm okay, Hovi. I'm all right." Corey winced as he picked up the washcloth and wiped away the thick grease from his body. It took some time. However, he persisted, and then lay down in the tub, to let the fresh-smelling water surround him.

What a nice bathtub. So big and white—just turn a knob and warm water flows in. This sure is different from the tin tub we use at home. It must be nice to be rich like Mrs. Chudzik. Why are some people rich while others are poor? he wondered.

Corey rolled over and over in the water. *My mom and dad are good folks. How come they have so little when we need so much with our big family? And here's Mrs. Chudzik, who doesn't have anyone but her dog, Hovi. She must be lonely. So I guess maybe we probably are better off than she is, except for the bathtub.*

Corey was comfortable by now, and he could have easily fallen asleep, except he slipped down deeper into the water, which lapped over his face. He yelped when the familiar dark memory jarred him awake. He struggled to sit up but slid again into the water.

Suddenly, the dog put his paws on the edge of the tub and barked, and before Corey could stop him, Hovi climbed into the tub with a *SPLASH*.

"Hovi, get out," Corey yelled, trying to stand. Then, with another *splash*, he sank under the water again.

The big dog, slipping and sliding, finally jumped out of the tub, taking more water than dog onto the floor and rug. Hovi shook the water from his bristly coat and waited for Corey to get out.

"Aw, Hovi. Why did you do that?" Corey asked.

Mrs. Chudzik knocked on the door. "Are you done yet? What's going on?"

"Woof!" Hovi barked.

"Yes, I'm done." Corey climbed out of the tub and stepped onto the soft but wet lambskin rug. He wrapped himself in the huge towel she'd given him and patted himself dry. Then he saw a tin of talcum powder on the table and shook it over himself, taking in the fresh scent.

After dressing in the clean clothes he'd brought, he combed his hair with an ivory comb he found on the table. "I'm done, Mrs. Chudzik," he called.

Mrs. Chudzik entered the bathroom and surveyed the flood damage. "What happened in here?"

"Hovi wanted a bath too," Corey said. "He climbed in with me."

"Oh no, he didn't want a bath. Hovi absolutely *hates* baths. He runs and hides when he hears the word. No, he was worried about you. He was trying to save you again."

Corey stroked Hovi's wet head as the dog lapped his face. "You are my hero, Hovi. You're a good boy."

"You must feel better now." Mrs. Chudzik picked up the towel and sopped up some of the water on the floor.

"Oh, lots better," Corey said. "I've never had a real bath in a real bathtub."

Mrs. Chudzik didn't say anything as she wrung out the towel. Then she pulled a jar from her pocket. "Now we'll put some of this healing salve that I made onto your hands. If you use it several times a day, your hands should heal within a week." She opened the jar and scooped out the creamy white ointment onto Corey's outstretched palms. "Does that feel better?"

"Yes, cool and better. Thank you." For a moment, Corey felt like crying.

Mrs. Chudzik gave him a long look—and then asked, "Now, do you want me to take you home? Or to the breaker?"

"What time is it?" Corey asked, brushing his eyes with his sleeve.

She looked at the clock on the wall. "It's half past three now. If we hurry, we can get you back to the breaker before it closes. You'll have a little time to work yet."

"But . . . I don't want . . ."

"Of course you don't. However, if you go back now, this whole incident will be behind you by tomorrow." She pushed him toward the door. "Out to the car. . . . Come on, hurry up. You'll get back in plenty of time. Just tell them you had to wash up." She stopped. "On second thought, you don't need to explain. Just go back to work."

"They'll never leave me alone."

Mrs. Chudzik stared at him with her frosty eyes. "They won't leave you alone and you'll never hear the end of it if you *don't* go back. And how will you explain it to your folks?" She picked up Corey's work clothes, which he'd left on the floor. "Do you have hot water at home? They'll need hot water and soap."

Corey nodded, but Mrs. Chudzik didn't notice. "You'll never get the grease out without hot water." She put everything in a laundry basket. "I'll use strong lye soap on this mess," she muttered. Then she opened the front door and shoved him out. "Come on; let's get you back there to the breaker before it closes."

Hovi darted eagerly out the door and hopped into the backseat of Mrs. Chudzik's automobile. Hovi appeared rock solid and regal as he glanced from right to left at the town passing by. No one would dare come near the automobile with Hovi—the appointed guardian of Mrs. Chudzik and her chariot—sitting proudly at the ready.

They dropped Corey off at the breaker. As he hurried into the breaker room, he realized that his disappearance wasn't noticed as much as his arrival with Mrs. Chudzik and Hovi. Some of the breaker boys saw him arrive in the big car, and Corey heard them buzzing as he headed back to work.

"Would ya look at that!" Frank exclaimed. "Look who's comin' back—and in a bee-utiful fancy auto."

Charlie, blocking Corey's path, muttered, "Well, *pardonnez* me!" Corey sidestepped him.

Paddy, a bandage over his nose, shook his head. "I'll be a monkey's uncle. He's in tight with that weird Chudzik lady."

The boss looked out the window. "Hey. Wait a minute, ain't that the new kid? Where has he been? How did he get a ride in a car like that?" When everyone tried to answer, he banged his stick on the floor and yelled, "Get to work!" The boys all scattered to their seats.

Corey went to the washroom and found his empty lunch pail where he had put it. He climbed into his seat at the breaker and began sorting the coal again. He was surprised that not another word was said about his lunch pail or the greasing he'd had—but the whispering went on about Corey's friendship with that creepy Chudzik lady and her hellhound.

21

Corey Talks Too Much

That evening before supper, Mom and Dad wanted to hear about Corey's first day at the breaker. So Corey told about his entire day—the greasing he received, the sore hands, Mrs. Chudzik to the rescue, and returning to the breaker in her automobile.

When he was finished, Mom spoke up. "Those boys are fierce! Imagine! Filling your trousers with that awful grease. And they ate your lunch too."

"They do that to everyone," Dad tried to explain. "It's like an initiation. They weren't picking on Corey particularly."

Mom turned to Dad accusingly. "You knew they would be shoving grease down his pants, and eating his lunch . . . and . . . ?" Her eyes flashed with annoyance. "How could you allow . . ."

"I didn't know they would do all that with the grease," Dad retorted. "I thought it would be some simple type of trick—yeah, like stealing his lunch, or hiding his hat. That's all they did to me."

"Now let me see your hands," Mom said. Corey stretched out his hands, and Mom gasped. "Oh, Corey, what a mess. Just look at the sores."

"They're feeling better now. Mrs. Chudzik gave me some ointment that she made herself."

"Mrs. Chudzik is an amazing woman," Mom said. "She should have been a doctor."

"She was a doctor when she lived in Poland," Corey told her, "but she is a nurse here."

"Well, I never knew that," Mom said. "It's a crime that people think terrible things about her."

Mom had made a special supper to celebrate Corey's first day of work—chicken with gravy, potatoes, and carrots. Corey was hungry and dug in eagerly, then winced with the pain from his hands and fingers. His mother took the fork and began to feed him.

"No, Mom. I can feed myself," Corey sputtered as she shoved chicken into his mouth.

Jack and Sammy kicked each other under the table and smothered their giggles.

"Stop it, Mom. I don't want you to feed me," Corey protested, grabbing the fork. "Mrs. Chudzik said my hands will heal in a week or so with the ointment." He pulled the jar out from his pocket and handed it to his mother.

She opened it and sniffed at the white cream inside.

"Mrs. Chudzik was very kind to you today," she said. "I must go over to her house and thank her."

"She's coming here to dinner on Sunday," Corey reminded her. "She'll bring back my clothes then."

Mom's eyes widened. "Please don't tell me you left your dirty, greasy clothes for Mrs. Chudzik to wash."

"She wanted to wash them—with lye soap and hot water."

"I am so embarrassed," Mom said, shaking her head. "I cannot believe you did that."

"Maybe she likes doing family washes," Corey argued. "Maybe she misses having a family."

"That might be true," Mom acknowledged. "She must be lonesome up in that big house with no one except her dog for companionship—and the whole town making fun of her, or scared of her." Mom's eyes suddenly filled with tears. "That wonderful, poor soul," she said. "We've got to do something. . . ."

"What do you think we should do?" Dad asked as he came back into the kitchen.

"We can be more neighborly and helpful. After all, she saved our son's life."

"I told Mrs. Chudzik I'd help her with her lawn this spring," Corey offered.

"That was nice of you, Corey," Mom said.

"Just be sure you do it," Dad said. "Don't conveniently forget."

"I won't forget," Corey answered, still not revealing how he actually owed Mrs. Chudzik that work to pay back the money she'd loaned him.

"How do you feel, Corey? Can you handle it at the breaker tomorrow?"

"Sure, I can handle it, Dad. Nobody bothered me this afternoon when I got back." He laughed. "They sure were surprised when they saw me in Mrs. Chudzik's Matheson Touring car."

The next day at work, some of the breaker boys were whispering and looking at Corey. He wondered why they were so obviously talking about him. Were they planning another grease attack? He was wary all day, watching out for Shorty with the grease can. But no one came after him. Yet the whispering and looks continued.

Finally, Charlie came over to Corey at lunchtime. "Hey, kid," he said, moving in closer. "We got a question for ya."

Corey, on guard, moved back. "Okay. Ask it."

"How well do ya know that old lady with the automobile?"

"I don't know her very well."

"Ya know her well enough to ride around with her in her fancy car."

"She saved my life, you know."

"No, we didn't know."

Corey began to tell about his close call with death and how Hovi saw him go under, and all that. The boys moved closer to hear the story. Corey nervously continued his tale, hardly noticing what details he was revealing, as he watched for an escape route, in case the boys were up to something. However, as he got into the story, the kids listened in rapt attention, without turning away. No one attempted to grease him or steal his lunch, or whatever they might have had in mind. He told them how it felt to be dead for a while. It was a fascinating story, and the breaker boys listened so intently that Corey embellished the tale. He described Hovi as a ferocious monster of a dog, and Mrs. Chudzik as peculiar and mysterious. Corey was enjoying his moment at center stage while all the breaker boys listened without poking fun or yelling nasty comments. When he finished, there was silence. The breaker boys were spellbound.

"Wow," said Charlie, in awe.

"Man alive," Paddy whispered.

"Then the rumors are all true," Frank said in amazement.

Corey suddenly felt sick. What had he done? He had been so captivated with the attention of his audience, he'd told them everything, including the part about Mrs. Chudzik and her coffin. He had betrayed her.

Corey burst out laughing. "You guys don't believe all that about the coffin, do ya? It never happened. I was just bamboozling ya." However, his laugh and his words did not ring true. The boys ignored him as they huddled together, whispering.

"What are you doing?" Corey demanded as he tried to elbow into the group. "What are you planning?"

"Aw, nothin', kid," Charlie said. "Get outta here."

22

Polish Night

O n Sunday evening, Corey's brother Jack came running into the house. "Dad! Mom! That lady is here."

"What lady?" Mom asked from the kitchen.

"You know, the one who saved Corey. The one with the automobile."

"Mrs. Chudzik, you mean. Of course she's here. We invited her to dinner."

"She's comin' up the walk, Mama," Sammy called as he watched from the parlor window.

"Come in, come in, Mrs. Chudzik," Dad was saying at the front door. "So happy you could come."

Mom and Corey hurried into the parlor.

Mrs. Chudzik was dressed up in a bright red cape-like coat that was the same shade as her red automobile.

Once again, Mrs. Chudzik nodded and stared at everyone in turn. Her gaze fell on Mom, and she extended her gloved hand. "Good evening, Mrs. Adamski."

Mom nodded and shook hands. "Please call me Annie. Welcome again to our house on this beautiful evening."

The lady then turned to Dad. "Mr. Adamski," she said politely, holding out her hand, which Dad took, after wiping his own hand off on his shirt.

Then she turned to the boys, who stood in a line, with their mouths open. Mrs. Chudzik had a look that intimidated people, especially kids.

"Hmm," she said. "You boys all look alike, don't you? Blond hair, blue eyes."

"No, I have brown eyes," Corey said. "Jack and Sammy have blue."

"Please come in and sit down, Mrs. Chudzik," said Mom. "Joe, take Mrs. Chudzik's coat."

"Where is Hovi?" Corey asked.

"I left him at home," she explained. "A Hovawart is always the guardian of the estate," she explained to Dad, who was taking her coat.

"Isn't Zerak the guardian?" Corey asked, remembering the grinning skeleton.

"Of the king, Corey," Mrs. Chudzik clarified. "Zerak is the guardian of the king, but Hovi is the guardian of the estate. There is a difference."

The mansion needs a guardian tonight while Mrs. Chudzik is gone, Corey thought. He was nervous about some of the breaker boys and what they might try to see if there really was a coffin in the parlor. Corey still felt to blame for arousing their curiosity by blabbing so much the other day.

"I've made a Polish dinner for this occasion," Mom said.

"Thank you very much, Mrs. Adam . . . Annie."

They all sat at the table. Dad inserted extra boards he'd made to expand it, so everyone could sit together. The grown-ups shared wine and Dad said, *"Smacznego!"* as they clinked their glasses.

"Oh, someone found pussy willows, I see," Mrs. Chudzik said, pointing to the bouquet the boys had picked in the woods that day.

"We did!" Jack and Sammy answered simultaneously.

Mom smiled. "A sure sign that spring is here, although a bit early, I think."

They sat down to *rosol*—Polish chicken soup served with noodles and greens. The main course was sausage, with Mom's delicious potato-and-cheese pierogi, and lots of mushrooms that Mom picked out in the woods last fall and dried.

It will be a long time before we have another big dinner like this, Corey thought. *Mom must have swapped cans of vegetables and jelly with Mrs. Sullivan in exchange for the chicken.* He had no idea where she might have found the sausage.

"How long have you been in America, Mrs. Chudzik?" Mom asked.

"A long time."

"You speak English with hardly a trace of a Polish accent," Mom noted.

"I tried hard to fit into the community," Mrs. Chudzik answered, looking away. "But it has been difficult—especially since my husband, Paul, died." She looked up at Corey. "Corey, what do you want to do, when you are all grown up? What type of work?"

"I'll probably be a miner, like Dad," he answered. "That's all we know and talk about."

"I wish our boys could learn something other than mining," Mom told her.

"How could we afford it? Miners don't make enough money to educate their kids." Dad caught Mom's warning look and added hastily, "It's not so bad now, since the unions have taken over. The hours and pay are better than they were when my father and Annie's father worked in the mines."

"And you, Corey, if you had a choice other than mining, what would you like to do or learn about?" Mrs. Chudzik asked.

Corey thought for a moment and then said, "I'd really love to know more how the earth began. Let me show you something." He excused himself and ran to his room. He had hidden the beautiful piece of coal Mr. Russell had given him in his cigar box. After retrieving it, he brought it back to the table and handed it to Mrs. Chudzik.

"Mr. Russell told me this leaf is from a tree that lived millions—maybe billions—of years ago. When I hold this rock in my hand, I wonder what was here on the earth back then. What dinosaurs or even people might have crawled around right here in Pennsylvania? It's a feeling that hits me here. . . ." He pointed to his chest. "It's kinda like when I look up at the stars on a clear night and know the light that I'm seeing left them millions of years ago."

Corey stopped talking and felt his face flush. He'd never told anyone about the wonder he felt when he held that fossil in his hand or looked up at the stars. "Um, I'd like you to have this," he said, handing the fossil to Mrs. Chudzik.

She took the coal and turned it over and over. "Thank you, Corey. This is a beautiful rock." She looked up at Mom and Dad and said, "Your son has a delightful sense of wonder and curiosity. The need to learn and under-stand is natural with creative, bright children like Corey."

Mom looked at Dad, then got up quickly and left the room. Corey wondered if he saw tears in her eyes.

Mrs. Chudzik polished the stone with her napkin, held it up to admire it again. "I will treasure your gift, Corey."

But when Mom came back into the room, the conver-sation about the future ended. Still, Mrs. Chudzik's ques-tion lingered in Corey's head.

Later, Mom placed her delicious *makowiec*—sweet poppy cake that she only made for important occasions—on the table. She cut it into narrow slices and placed them on plates.

"You must be Polish too," Mrs. Chudzik said to Mom. "You certainly know how to cook like us."

"I learned from Joe's mother, but I was born in Wales. My father worked in the coalfields in southern Wales. He came over here to work when I was about ten years old. Mom and I joined him later. Next time you come, I'll cook a Welsh dinner—perhaps Welsh *cawl.*" She paused and looked down, embarrassed. "I don't cook with lamb here, but it tastes fine with gammon—pork," she explained.

Pork is cheaper than lamb, Corey thought.

Mrs. Chudzik was quiet for a moment, then said, "I notice you said 'next time' I come . . . ," Mrs. Chudzik responded. "Will I be lucky enough to be invited again?"

"Of course you will," Mom promised, putting her arm around Mrs. Chudzik's shoulder. "Many more times."

Mrs. Chudzik's face brightened. "Oh . . . oh, that will be delightful."

"Tell us about your life in Poland," Dad said as he passed the plates of poppy cake. "We heard you were a doctor."

"I still am," Mrs. Chudzik answered. "Well, I feel I will always be a doctor, even though I don't have a license here in Pennsylvania." Her shoulders dropped. "It saddens me that my work and studies in Europe are not recognized here."

"What kind of medicine did you practice in the old country?" Mom asked.

"I was privileged to study with a brilliant woman obstetrician, Anna Tomaszewicz-Dobrska."

"Oh, an obstetrician . . . a doctor who delivers babies," Mom said.

"Yes, Annie. I was hoping to be able to help midwives and mothers here in America."

Corey noticed a look between the two women—and a knowing smile. *Does Mrs. Chudzik know that Mom is going to have a baby? How could she know?*

Mrs. Chudzik continued, "Dr. Dobrska also studied psychiatry, which is a fairly new field of medicine. For several years, she worked with a famous psychiatrist in Zurich's hospital for the mentally ill. I was able to learn a lot from Dr. Dobrska as her colleague."

"You worked with mentally ill patients too?" Dad asked. "That's the kind of disease that people don't own up to—or talk about."

"It was thought at one time that seriously ill mental patients were hopeless, but we found that many could be helped." She smiled sadly. "So you see, I had a good, rounded education as her colleague. However, it seems I will never be able to help people here in America."

"It is our loss, Mrs. Chudzik," Mom said, reaching across the table and touching Mrs. Chudzik's hand.

Later that evening, Mrs. Chudzik recited an old Polish fairy tale for the boys, about pussy willows and how they came to be. She even joined the family singing Polish folk songs.

Corey almost forgot about the boys from the mine and what they might be planning. He would find out soon enough!

23
Hogwash!

Corey could not sleep Sunday night. He tossed and turned, thinking of all the things Mrs. Chudzik said about discovery and wonder, and about bright, creative children—*like him!* It was hard to imagine himself ever becoming a scientist or an engineer. That meant going to schools and colleges, which was impossible. He would never find the answers to the beginnings of the planet and life and things. His existence would be the same as his Dad's and both his grandfathers'—in the mines. And that was that!

He was tired and sleepy Monday. When the morning whistle blew, he dragged himself from bed to work.

The older boys at the breaker were acting strange. Charlie, Paddy, and Frank stuck together like glue all day.

Once again, they whispered to one another and stole curious looks at Corey.

What is going on? Corey wondered. Whatever they were talking about, or what it was they had done or were about to do, he hoped it had nothing to do with Mrs. Chudzik. Finally, at lunch, once they had finished eating and were outside, Charlie, Frank, and Paddy came over to Corey.

"So, did you get to go out ridin' around in that fancy car this past weekend?" Charlie asked Corey.

"No, but Mrs. Chudzik came over to our house for supper last night—in her touring car, of course," Corey offered. He loved to see their amazement that Corey was actually friends with the rich, eccentric, and standoffish widow, and had even ridden in her automobile.

"Aha! Did ya hear that, boys?" Charlie said to his friends. "The lady was over to Corey's house for Sunday dinner."

"So that's where she was. At the kid's house," Frank said.

"Were you going to call on Mrs. Chudzik?" Corey asked. "Or are you schemin' up something to do to her?"

"Naw, course not," Charlie answered. "We're just curious."

"We've heard a lot of creepy stories about the lady, not just from you," Frank said. "Everybody says she's peculiar. So we decided we would go make a call on her. We hoped she'd invite us into her parlor."

"We were gonna say we're good friends of yours," Paddy added. "Since you and her are such good pals."

"You are not good friends of mine—and I am not her *pal*. She saved my life and she's a nice lady," Corey stated emphatically. In a softer voice, he asked, "So, what happened at her house?"

"We knocked on the front door like any good neighbor—"

Paddy interrupted Charlie. "That knocker could've raised the dead. And maybe it did! 'Cause the next thing we hear is that big wild dog of hers barking and howling at us."

"Yeah, that howl gave me the creeps," said Charlie.

"He was inside that door scratchin' and growlin'," Frank said. "Just waitin' to tear us to pieces."

"Did you leave then?" Corey asked, hoping that was the end of the story.

"Paddy was ready to run off," Frank said scornfully.

"We didn't want to leave after goin' all the way over to her part of town, so we decided to take a look inside," Charlie explained. "We wanted to see if the stories were true . . . you know . . . about the coffin in the parlor."

Corey gulped. "Did you guys break into Mrs. Chudzik's house? All because I told you a crazy story? I told you it was hogwash."

Charlie was insulted. "No, we wouldn't break in. We are good, churchgoin' Catholics. We would never do stuff like breakin' into that old widow's house. All we decided to do, since she wasn't home, was to peek in a window."

Frank nodded. "We saw a window that was lit up on the side of the house."

"Mrs. Chudzik has electricity. Ain't that somethin'?"

Paddy interrupted. "We all use kerosene lanterns, but she has *electricity.*"

"The window was close enough to the ground that we figured we could climb up and at least look inside."

"So?" Corey tried to picture just which room they were looking in.

"I stood under the window and boosted Paddy up to look inside—since he's the smallest," Charlie said.

The boys glanced at one another. "Corey won't believe us," Paddy said. "Nobody will believe us."

Charlie continued. "Paddy got up to the window and looked in, and he was so scared he screamed. . . ."

"No, I did not scream," Paddy insisted. "And I wasn't scared."

"Oh, you screamed, all right," Charlie maintained.

"For Pete's sake. What did you see, Paddy?" Corey asked. "Get on with it."

"Well, since Paddy was so scared he couldn't talk, Frank lifted *me* up," Charlie told him. "And I saw it too."

"Charlie was just as scared as me," Paddy said accusingly. "All he could do was point to the window and stutter."

"I never stuttered," Charlie snapped.

"Then it was my turn," Frank said. "Charlie boosted me, but he was shaking so hard I thought he would drop me, so I only got a quick glance in the window."

"So you never got to see a coffin, did you?" Corey said hopefully. "I told you. . . ."

"No, we did not see the coffin. But we did see a skeleton," Frank insisted.

Corey laughed as he visualized Zerak grinning at the three terrified boys. "Sure you did."

"Don't laugh. We really saw it—all three of us," Charlie affirmed. "A real, live skeleton."

"No question about it. There was a skeleton," said Frank. "And it's not funny, Corey."

"So you all saw a real, live skeleton." Corey could not speak for a moment, then he said, "You know that's a story no one will ever believe."

"Well, we did see it," Charlie insisted. "And it was most definitely a skeleton."

Paddy nodded. "And it wore a miner's hat."

"You saw a real, live skeleton in a miner's hat," Corey said, laughing even harder.

"Don't you believe us?" Frank asked.

"Yeah, sure." Corey started to walk away. "Sure I believe you."

"Corey, you of anyone should believe it's true. You saw a coffin and we saw a skeleton. It's all true," Paddy said. "All the things we've heard about Mrs. Chudzik."

"Yeah, a real, live skeleton wearing a hat, and a coffin in the parlor!" Corey shook his head. "Nobody with a brain in their head would believe a story like yours. And nobody with a brain in their head would believe a story like mine, either." He walked away. "It's all a lot of hogwash!"

24
Brawl

On his way home from work on Monday, Corey met Anthony coming toward him. "Hey, Corey. I'm startin' work at the breaker Tuesday—tomorrow!"

"Good!" Corey called back. "But you'd better be prepared. Remember what happened to me on my first day."

As they walked along together, they made plans to outwit the breaker boys. "We'll put your lunch in with mine in my lunch pail. They haven't touched mine since my first day," Corey suggested.

"Sounds like a good plan," Anthony agreed.

"We'll eat our lunch out in back of the fence that separates the breaker from the office building," Corey said. "They'll never know where you went." He chuckled at the thought of outwitting Charlie and his friends.

✢ ✢ ✢

On Tuesday, as predicted, the boys found Anthony's lunch pail and hid it. The joke was on them, because Corey and Anthony had eaten their lunch, and the boys who found the pail were probably disappointed that it was empty. Corey and Anthony had a good laugh. Anthony never got the greasing that Corey had to endure, but he did suffer painful, bleeding sores on his hands.

Anthony cringed as he washed his hands in the washroom. "I have some good ointment to put on that," Corey told him, taking the small jar of ointment from his pocket.

"Hey, where can I get that stuff?" Charlie asked, watching as Corey smeared the salve on Anthony's hands and fingers.

"You can't buy it in a store," Corey told him. "Mrs. Chudzik made it for me."

"Oh, really?" Charlie said, coming closer. "Is it her own homemade remedy?"

"It's soothing, and then the cuts and bruises go away in a short while," Corey said. "I think it toughens your hands too, so they don't get as sore anymore."

"Look at this." Anthony held up his hands. "The redness is almost gone already."

"Well, now we know for sure," Charlie announced as he grabbed the jar of ointment from Corey and held it up for all to see. "Mrs. Chudzik is a witch!"

"Mrs. Chudzik is a *doctor*," Corey said, trying to seize the jar. "Stop spreading those stupid rumors about her!"

"Then she's a witch doctor! And you're gonna become

a warlock," Charlie yelled for everyone to hear.

Corey grabbed hold of Charlie's sleeve and pulled him closer. "You ugly goop! You and your friends got nothin' to do but make fun of an old lady and peek in her window at night."

Charlie threw the jar across the room, where it dropped onto the floor and shattered.

"Now look what you've done," Corey yelled as he pushed Charlie hard in the chest, knocking him to the ground.

Charlie didn't move for a moment, then rolled over, breathing hard. "You knocked the breath outta me. I'm gonna get you for that!" He pulled himself up and was about to clobber Corey, when—*SMACK!* Corey beat him to the punch with another blow to the chest. By now most of the boys were taking sides and punching one another.

"FIGHT! FIGHT!"

The boss burst into the room, looking from one to another at the fighting boys, wondering who to blame for the riot. Then he grabbed his stick and set to whacking the brawlers. "Stop it! Knock it off!" he yelled with each blow. "You'll all be penalized for this! Get back to work before you lose your jobs!"

After a few minutes, the fight came to an end, but there were only a few breaker boys without a black eye or a bloody nose.

25
Truce

Both Anthony and Corey had bruises and bloodshot eyes and hurt all over where the boys had punched them. The fight stopped, but Charlie, Frank, and Paddy and their pals hollered all afternoon that they would get even. Finally, after an hour's lecture on fighting by Mr. McBride in the main office, the boys who took part in the squabble got sent home early and had their pay docked.

Corey decided he wouldn't go home yet. He'd walk along with Anthony.

"Want to come with me to see Mrs. Chudzik?" Corey asked. "She might have more of that ointment. You'll see what a great lady she is."

Anthony shook his head. "I just want to go home. I'm hurting from the fight, and my hands are killin' me.

Now I'm thinkin' I might work as a spragger instead of a breaker boy."

"You need to make up your mind that no job at the mine is perfect. Besides, not all the breaker boys are bad eggs," Corey said. "It's just those few who think they're the big cheese . . . like Charlie and Paddy. . . ."

"Yeah, yeah, I know. I've had enough of them."

"They didn't grease you, like they did to me, and I didn't quit," Corey reminded him. "I'll bet you by tomorrow they'll be over this fight and won't even remember what it was about."

"Just the same, I don't like what happened today, and I think I'd like to be a spragger instead of a breaker boy. Besides, spraggers get more money. I'm gonna talk to my pa tonight about switching jobs." He ran down the hill to his house.

Corey kicked a stone as he recalled his ride down the chute with Mr. McBride. He would never get a job down in the mine. Not after that day.

He thought about becoming a spragger too. Spraggers needed to be fast and nimble. Anthony was fast. He always won races in the Labor Day games and probably would do well as a spragger.

A spragger would run alongside the speeding coal cars and insert sprags into the wheels, which would act like brakes until the cars stopped. He recalled that one of his school chums who became a spragger wasn't nimble enough or fast enough and lost his hand in the spokes of a fast-moving car. Corey was good with his hands, but he would probably fall flat on his face if he raced one of the coal carts. Besides, that job was deep inside the mine.

It was no use—he couldn't change jobs until he got over the phobia, and that might never happen. He'd just have to get along with Charlie and his sidekicks. The other breaker boys never caused any trouble—unless Charlie egged them on.

He heard footsteps behind him. Looking over his shoulder, he saw Charlie, Paddy, and Frank coming his way. This was not the route they usually took to go home.

Frank called, "Hey, Corey. Wait up."

Corey wondered what he should do. If he ran, he'd look like a sissy. If he stopped, Frank, Paddy, and Charlie might just clobber him again. He took a chance and slowed down, swaggering a little so at least he wouldn't appear to be scared.

"Look, I don't want to fight anymore," he told the boys in a calm voice.

"Hey, neither do we. Let's call a truce, okay?" Charlie held out his hand. "We have more important things to think about."

"Like what?" Corey shook Charlie's hand warily.

"Ain't ya heard?" Charlie said. "Everything is half price at Sans Souci Park this weekend. It's got somethin' to do with raising money for the new hospital. I heard the mine is payin' the other half."

"Yeah, can ya believe the mine doin' that?" Paddy butted in.

Frank rolled his eyes. "They like to look good in the community."

"We're all goin'. Are you?" Charlie asked.

"I wish I could. I love goin' to Sans Souci Park. But I can't. If there's no work, I have to stick around and help my mother. Why are you asking me?"

"Before you say no, listen to me. There's gonna be an exhibition ball game between the two best breaker boy teams on Sunday at the field next to the carnival."

"It's to raise money for the hospital too," Paddy cut in.

Charlie rolled his eyes. "Never mind all that. Listen, kid. That friend of yours, Anthony? He says the two of you are good players—that he's a good pitcher, and you're a good hitter. So let's throw all our rows and quarrels aside and get a good team together. Whadda ya say?"

Frank spoke up. "The Black Gold Colliery breaker boys beat us for the championship last year."

"We would've won, but some of our best players moved away," Paddy added.

"We're gonna have tryouts Saturday afternoon at the field next to the park," Charlie said, ignoring the interruptions. "So, are you in?"

"Well, yeah, but . . ." Corey really wanted to be on the team but wasn't sure if Mom would need him at home on Sunday.

"Oh, come on," Charlie begged. "We need fresh new players. We want to smash the other team on Sunday and get set up for the season."

"Okay, I'll try out, but I'm not sure if I'll be goin' to Sans Souci Park this weekend," Corey repeated.

"Never mind tryin' out if you ain't goin' to play," Charlie said, spitting on the ground. "We need players who'll be there at every game." He turned on his heel and walked away, with his pals tagging along behind.

26

Knockers?

Corey continued on his way, thinking about the ball team. It would be fun to be on a championship team. Even Dad hoped Corey would make the team. No matter how bad the work was, looking forward to playing baseball on a team made the job of a breaker boy bearable. Yes, he'd try out for the team and make sure he'd play on Sunday at the park.

Corey soon came to Abby's shortcut to Mrs. Chudzik's and paused for a moment when he saw the gaping entrance to the old mine at the bottom of the cliff. He hadn't panicked the day he waited by the cave entry while Dad and Mr. Russell went inside. What would happen if he went in a little way today, by himself? Would it work today? Why not give it a try?

He headed toward the face of the cliff. The air was fresh and a gentle breeze brought that pleasant scent of pine trees. He'd be fine. He wouldn't go far into the mine. He couldn't, anyway, since it was blocked from a cave-in years ago. He'd stay calm if he walked just a short way into the tunnel.

When he approached the opening, a gust of cool wind chilled him. He took a deep breath. "I am all right. Just lookin' around," he told himself casually. "I don't have to stay. I can leave whenever I want." He remembered that he must believe those words, or they wouldn't work. So he thought them again, concentrating on each one, as he went into the cave.

The opening of the mine was huge, and there was plenty of room to walk around, just as he remembered. Maybe he could go a little farther—just a few feet or so. He was not afraid. There was nothing at all to be afraid of.

He walked to the passageway near the back wall and headed even deeper into the mountain. He could still stand up and move around, but now the way was cluttered with boulders and dirt.

Corey had to climb over some of the boulders that had fallen. *I'll just do ten more steps, and then I'll leave*, he decided.

One, two, three, four, five. The pathway was tighter now, and he could see only darkness ahead—or was it a wall of stone? He mustn't concentrate on the shadows or the cluttered passage. He would think only of the next five steps and then he would leave.

Six, seven, eight, nine, ten.

He did it! Next time he'd go for fifteen steps, and after that he'd aim for twenty. That's how Mrs. Chudzik said it would work. Corey was about to turn and leave, when suddenly he heard something.

Knock. Knock. Knock.

It was coming from deep within the old mine, and he stopped walking. *What could it be? No one has worked this mine in fifty years or more.*

Knock. Knock. Knock.

It was faint and faraway. But it was real and it was as if the mountain itself was sending a message—a warning. Abby had heard knocking when she'd been caught in the pipe. The knockers. They were known to warn of cave-ins.

I won't let that old tale frighten me. This tunnel has existed for years, and the cave-in was long ago. There's a cause of the knocking, and it's not fairy-tale elves. I'll stay calm. I'm not afraid. I can choose to leave whenever I want.

KNOCK! KNOCK!

And . . . I choose to leave right now!

Corey turned around in the narrow passageway and then bolted back to the bright sunshine outside.

Corey bounded toward Mrs. Chudzik's house to tell her his news, when he saw Abby in her front yard.

He raced over to ask her if she had told anyone about what really happened up on the cliff. "Hey, Abby, how are you?" he asked as he approached her. "I haven't seen you since you fell into the pipe."

"I'm fine," she said. "Papa said you helped him find the pipe the next day."

"Uh-huh." Corey switched from one foot to the other. "Abby, did you tell your father what happened up there? About me, I mean. How I wasn't any help at all."

"I made up my mind I wouldn't tell anyone what happened to you, and I didn't."

"I came over the next morning to apologize to your folks, but your dad and mom were so nice to me, I wasn't sure whether they knew or not, so I didn't say anything."

"No one knows except you and me, Corey."

Corey hated to even remember that awful day, let alone talk about it with anyone. He drew a letter C on the ground, with the toe of his boot. "I guess it's better not to say anything to anyone, now that it's over, anyway. I hope I can make it up to you someday."

"I hope that you'll get better someday." She turned to go back into her house.

"Wait." Corey took hold of Abby's arm. "I am being treated for my sickness."

"You are?"

"Mrs. Chudzik is helping me. I went into the entrance to the old mine—just a few minutes ago—and followed the tunnel a short way. I didn't panic or get sick. Next time I'll go in deeper."

"I'm glad you're getting help, Corey." She turned to walk away again.

"I heard the knockers while I was there."

"Did you?" Abby wheeled around. "I heard them when

I was down in the pipe." She paused for a minute, then headed to the back door.

Corey called to her. "Are we still friends?"

Abby didn't answer.

Feeling gloomy, he headed to Mrs. Chudzik's house. He hoped Abby would forgive him, especially since she'd seen how helpless he'd been up there on the mountain. He must have looked dim-witted, clinging to that tree.

Just then he heard Abby call out, "Corey! Corey!"

He stopped and looked back. "What?"

"We're still friends."

Before he could answer, Abby scooted into her house.

27

Off-Limits

Hovi's throaty, fierce bark and the clicking of his paws on the hardwood floor were familiar to Corey by now. *Most folks would beeline it out of here in a flash and never know what a sweet dog he really is,* Corey thought.

The door opened and Mrs. Chudzik peered out. She had her glasses on and her eyes looked huge.

Hovi pushed her aside with his nose and, as usual, jumped on Corey, lapping his face.

"Down, boy," Corey said as Hovi jumped again, nuzzling his nose under Corey's chin.

"Down, Hovi," Mrs. Chudzik commanded. The dog sat, but his tail wagged furiously. "Now, Corey. Are you in some kind of trouble again?"

"No. I came to tell you that I went a little way into the

old mine today, and I told myself that I was fine, that nothing could hurt me. I did all the things you told me, and I didn't panic. I think I'm going to be better."

"Well, that's a good start and shows you can be stronger than those fears." She opened the door wide and motioned him in. "Come in. No need to stand at the door."

Corey went into the house. "I know my phobia won't go away real quick, but I thought it was a good start too."

"Be careful not to go into the mine too far just to try things out. One never knows what might be going on inside the mountain, like flooding or black damp—you know, deadly gas." She paused, thinking. "Here you are trying to get over your phobia, and here I am talking about danger in the mine. That doesn't make sense, does it?"

"No one can get into the mine that way, Mrs. Chudzik. The tunnel to the gangway is blocked with boulders and rocks." Corey followed her into the kitchen with Hovi at his heels, then sat at his usual place at the table. Hovi settled down on the floor near him.

"Now, tell me what happened at the old mine today," she said, and sat opposite him.

Corey related how he'd recited the positive words over and over. "I kept telling myself I was in control, and I wasn't afraid and could leave whenever I wanted."

"And how did you feel?"

"I felt fine. Like you said, I took deep breaths and walked just ten steps into the tunnel. That was all. Next time I'll do fifteen steps. And then twenty . . . a little at a time." Corey smiled. "I think—*I know*—that I'll get over the panicky feeling, and maybe the dreams, too, if I keep doing what you said."

"Well, ten steps is a big accomplishment. Some people might take only two steps to start.

"I went into town today and made an arrangement to have the mine closed up tight. They will seal up the entrance and the pipe sometime next week." Mrs. Chudzik poured water into the kettle and placed it on a burner. "I have decided to have milk and biscuits. You may join me if you want, but first, you must wash your hands."

Corey could feel his face flush as he looked down at the coal dust, dirt, and blood from the fight that encrusted his hands, fingers, and nails. "I'm sorry, Mrs. Chudzik. I haven't been home yet."

She turned on the tap and placed a towel by the sink. "Wash up," she said as she took milk from the icebox and poured two glasses.

Corey was mortified as he soaped his hands and held his breath when they stung. After washing his hands and face, he looked at the once-clean towel, now black with coal dust and dirt.

Mrs. Chudzik was watching him. "Well, are you going to tell me or not?"

"Tell you what?" Corey asked.

"You were obviously in a fight today. Black eyes and bruises don't appear out of nowhere."

"Some of the breaker boys ganged up on me."

"Why?" Mrs. Chudzik sat at the table again and took off her thick glasses. "I am waiting to hear the story."

How could he ever tell Mrs. Chudzik that the boys broke the jar of ointment and claimed Mrs. Chudzik was a witch? How could he explain that that's what the fight was about?

Instead he said, "I can't remember just what started it, but the boss came in and stopped it, and it's all over now. Sometimes right in the middle of a fight, the boys get another idea in their heads and move on to something else. Then they forget to be mad. In fact, the boys that fought with me asked me to try out for the baseball team on Saturday."

"Fight and then forget. I suppose that's better than holding a grudge forever." She put biscuits and jam on the table. "Best thing to do when there's a fight is to mind your own business and walk away *before* arguments turn into fights. That's what I do. I stay away from things that don't concern me. I have also found that people can be cruel; it's easier to have nothing to do with anyone." Then Mrs. Chudzik asked, "How is your mother, Corey? Isn't the baby due soon?"

"Yes, very soon."

"I'm sure everything will be fine. She's already had three healthy babies."

Corey was about to smear jam on his biscuit but stopped—the knife in midair. "Why wouldn't she be fine? Mom says that women are made to have babies."

"Of course they are, and your mother is right. Perhaps you will have a baby sister next time I see you."

Corey continued spreading the jam and stuffed the

biscuit into his mouth. He was about to leave when Mrs. Chudzik looked at the clock.

"Why don't I drive you home? It's getting late, and we don't want your mother to be worried—especially now." She got up and took her keys from a hook. I'll meet you out in the driveway, Corey. You go ahead while I get my purse."

Hovi got up, stretched, and looked at Mrs. Chudzik expectantly, his tail wagging. "He knows when I get my purse that he's going to take a ride," she explained.

Corey walked down the hallway toward the front door, when he realized the parlor door was open. He paused to peek into the dark room. The coffin was still there, resting on tall, heavy pedestals. Both the coffin and the stands were made of ebony or another black wood and carved with terrifying figures. He'd never noticed the forms the night he almost drowned. He tiptoed into the parlor to take a better look.

Snakes, with fangs ready to strike, wound around carved vines on the coffin and the pedestals; a bat, wings outstretched and a dead mouse in its mouth, guarded the head of the coffin; skulls grinned at him from the corners. Smaller images of angels and demons filled in every space.

Corey shuddered at the gruesome sculptures, unaware Mrs. Chudzik had come into the parlor. He recoiled when he heard her ask in a hostile voice, "What are you doing in here?"

28

The Reason Why

Corey wheeled around to see Mrs. Chudzik standing with her arms folded across her chest, glaring at him. "I . . . wanted to see the . . . things on the coffin . . . the snakes and stuff. I don't remember noticing them the night I almost drowned."

"Are you satisfied now?"

"Uh-huh. I guess so," Corey answered in a shaky voice. "I just kinda wondered . . ."

"Wondered what?"

"Why . . . you sleep in that coffin?" There, he couldn't believe he said it right out. As he watched Mrs. Chudzik's eyes darken, and her mouth tighten into a thin line, a cold fear crept over him. Goose bumps prickled his arms and neck. Was he about to see her turn into that creature everyone believed her to be?

"I do *not* sleep in that coffin." The words spit out of her mouth.

"But . . . but I saw you in there that night." Corey couldn't stop himself. It was as if suddenly all the questions he had, needed answers *right now*.

Mrs. Chudzik remained silent.

He swallowed hard. "Did I dream it—when I was unconscious?"

Mrs. Chudzik pointed to the door. "Get in the car."

As Corey followed her, he felt sick. She'd saved his life, and helped him in a dozen other ways. Now he could tell she was furious. *Why did I ask those questions? Now I've ruined our friendship.*

Hovi jumped into the back while Mrs. Chudzik and Corey got into the car's front seats. She started up the engine and, without a word, propelled out of the driveway and down the street.

After a few minutes, Corey couldn't stand the silence between them any longer. "Mrs. Chudzik? I'm sorry I went into the parlor. I was in there before, and I didn't think you would mind."

She looked straight ahead and didn't answer.

"Please don't be mad at me," he pleaded. "I'd feel awful bad if we aren't friends anymore." He looked away and watched the blurry trees go by, remembering the tree he had clutched up on the cliff. It had been rigid and unbending, but he'd clung to it anyway and felt protected. "I don't care one whit that you have a coffin in the parlor."

Corey felt Hovi's tongue lapping his neck from the backseat. At least Hovi still cared about him.

Mrs. Chudzik pulled the car over to the side of the road, stopped the engine, and turned to him. "I understand you have questions about the coffin," she said in a softer voice. "I know it's not normal to keep something like that in the parlor."

"Lots of kids ask me about it, since they saw me ride in your car."

"What do you tell them?"

"I say that I don't know anything and it's none of their business why you keep the coffin in your parlor. I tell them that you saved my life. But they think I'm lying, and . . . well, that's what the fight was about."

"I think it's time you have some answers, Corey. I don't want you to fight over our friendship.

"It's all about sadness," she said, clasping her hands. "When my husband, Paul, brought me to this country, we never thought it would matter that I was from Poland and spoke little English. I hoped my license to practice as a doctor would be recognized. But it wasn't. The people in the town loved Dr. Chudzik—Paul—and they welcomed me, too. After all, the mining families here were from Poland, Czechoslovakia . . . everywhere. And most of them didn't speak English either. I was granted my license as a nurse as long as I practiced directly under a doctor. So I was able to help the miners and their families, but always at Paul's side."

There was a silence while Mrs. Chudzik looked off, as if remembering. Corey noticed her face soften and she looked younger.

"When Paul died, I was completely alone and abandoned. I missed him so much that I thought I would die. In fact, I hoped I would die." She put her hands to her face. After a moment, she went on. "You see, no one came to comfort me. I was totally alone. I withdrew from the community, which I felt had discarded me. I hid from everyone, except for Hovi." She leaned back and patted the dog's head. "I had the coffin put into my parlor. When I needed to be near Paul, I would lie in the coffin and think about him and how someday I hoped we'd be together again."

She looked at Corey and he thought he saw tears in her eyes. "It was a comfort for me to be near him. I don't *sleep* there. I *pray* there."

Corey didn't know what to say, but he understood.

It was sad to think no one had cared about her when she needed people to care. Instead, they'd left her all alone, after all the good things Dr. Chudzik had done for the miners and the people in the town.

"So now you know. I've never told anyone. Yes, you did see me in the coffin. I'm sure it frightened you when you walked in that night. It's a favorite topic in the town's gossip."

Corey nodded. "Yes, it is." *There's a lot more gossip about Mrs. Chudzik and Hovi than that.* But Corey wouldn't tell her that right now. Maybe not ever.

"Corey, one reason I felt comfortable with you is that

you never asked me about anything. You and your family accepted me just the way I am. . . ."

"I hate it when people talk about you, because they don't know you at all. I think if people knew you, they'd love you like we all do."

"You all love me?" Mrs. Chudzik's eyes widened in amazement.

"Yes, my whole family. I think—*I know*—that others would love you too, if you'd let them in."

"Let them into my house? Never."

"I mean . . . into your . . . your life." Corey found it hard to explain what he meant. Then he suddenly wondered, *Could Mrs. Chudzik have a phobia? Is she afraid too?*

Mrs. Chudzik started the car up again. "Let's take you home now."

29
Too Many Questions

That evening, before Corey went to bed, he told his parents about his visit to the mine entrance and how he heard the same knocking that Abby heard when she was in the pipe on the top of the cliff. "What could it have been?"

"The knockers, of course," Mom said with a laugh. "What else?" Then she got serious. "You know the knockers warn of cave-ins—so you'd better stay away from that old mine."

Dad gave Mom a warning look. "That's a tale from the old countries, Annie. You know how hard Corey is trying to get over his phobia—or whatever it's called. For Pete's sake, don't scare him with the stories of the knockers."

"My father told me stories about the knockers in

Wales," Mom said, ignoring him. "Like the time—"

Dad interrupted. "Stop it, Annie!"

Corey could tell there might be an argument starting. He might need to walk away, like Mrs. Chudzik said. He cleared his throat. "I only wanted to tell you how I am trying to get well, and it's working." He went on to describe how he went a little way into the mine and had no fear because he was only doing a little at a time, and telling himself he could leave whenever he wanted. "I didn't go far, Mom," he said. "Just ten steps, and that's all. Next time I'll go fifteen steps. Lots of fears can be stopped this way. Mrs. Chudzik told me so, and she knows a lot."

"Well, that's a good thing," Mom said. "Mrs. Chudzik is very kind to you, Corey. She's saved your life, and she continues to help you and care about you." Mom's mouth quivered like it often did when she was sad. "I wish I could help you like she does."

"You do, Mom, when you're not too busy," Corey said quickly. "Mrs. Chudzik asked about you. She wondered when the baby was due."

Mom looked away. "I think you're over at Mrs. Chudzik's too often. You shouldn't pester her like you do."

"I don't pester her. She likes me to visit. I don't think anyone ever visits her." Corey was sure an argument was brewing in Mom's mind, so he said, "I'm so tired. I think I'll go to bed now." He yawned a fake yawn.

"Wait one minute," Mom said. "You haven't told us where you got the bruises."

"We've been waiting for you to tell us," Dad said, "and

we're still waiting to hear where you got the money for the gifts."

"You promised you wouldn't ask about that. Remember? A deal's a deal," Corey said firmly. "But I *will* tell you about my black eye. Charlie gave it to me. He's always lookin' for trouble. There was a brawl in the breaker today. It's over now, and I'm fine." He kissed his mother good night and headed for the stairs. "Don't worry." He ran up the steps, two at a time. He needed to get away from the explosion that he believed was about to happen.

His brothers were in bed and already asleep. They lay on the bed sideways, and after he got into his pajamas, he climbed in between them. Sammy rolled over and smacked Corey in the face with his arm. Corey winced as his eye smarted again. He wished he had a bed to himself. Now that there was another baby coming, would they have to sleep four to a bed?

He could hear his mother and father arguing downstairs and wondered why Mrs. Chudzik's name was mentioned over and over. Then he heard Dad say, "I think you're jealous of Mrs. Chudzik's attention to Corey."

"Maybe I am!" Mom wailed. "She's a better mother to him than I am." She burst into tears and sobbed for several minutes.

"Annie, you're worn-out and upset. Nobody is a better mom than you."

His dad's voice was comforting now, and as their voices became quiet, Corey slowly fell asleep.

30
Sans Souci Park

On Friday night, Corey thought he heard women's voices downstairs, but he was just too tired to care. At least it wasn't one of his scary dreams. He adjusted his pillow and went back to sleep.

But when Saturday morning came, as soon as Corey opened his eyes, he wondered, *Did Mom have the baby? Is that why I heard voices most of the night?* He needed to know, but the house was quiet now.

Corey slipped downstairs in his pajamas. Dad was drinking coffee at the kitchen table.

"What's going on? I heard voices during the night. Did Mom have the baby yet?"

"You slept through all the excitement," Dad said. "Mom thought the baby was coming. I asked Mrs. Balaski to come over, and she brought two neighbor ladies. They got the fire going and sterilized everything in boiling water. But the baby didn't come, so they made breakfast for all of us before they went home. It's in the oven." Dad went to the kitchen door and opened it wide.

"That's why it's so hot in here." Corey sat at the table. "Where's Mom now?"

"She's sleeping. It was a false alarm, but the women feel sure the baby will come any day now." Dad poured more coffee from the pot on the coal stove.

"So what can I do today to help?" Corey knew that the boys might be in the way while the baby was coming. He recalled that when they were born, he was moved from one neighborhood house to another.

Dad thought for a moment. "It would be better if the boys weren't around today. Things could get busy and they might be underfoot."

"Everything is half price at Sans Souci today. Could I take the boys?" Corey suggested. "We'd be gone all day."

"That sounds like a good idea," Dad said.

"Okay," Corey agreed. "I'll take them."

Dad took a coffee can from the shelf behind the stove and opened it. "Here's money for all of you. You can buy hot dogs for lunch. Come home before dark. That means you leave the carnival at least an hour before dark. It's a good hour's walk each way." He pulled out two bills and handed them to Corey.

Corey and his father ate the egg, potato, and cheese casserole Mrs. Balaski had made, saving some for the rest of the family. "I don't know if Mom will want to eat," Dad said, "but she needs her strength."

Corey took the money and went upstairs to wake Jack and Sammy. *They'll be crazy with excitement,* he thought as he nudged his brothers. "Time to get up."

"No, I don't want to go to school," Jack muttered, pulling the pillow over his head.

"You don't have to go to school. It's Saturday," Corey reminded them. "Come on. Get up and have breakfast."

"Why?" Sammy whined. "If it's Saturday, why are you waking us up? Has Mom had the baby yet?"

Jack popped up from under the covers. "Yeah, do we have a new brother?"

"Not yet."

"Then I'm not getting up," Jack said.

"If you don't get up and get dressed, I guess you don't want to come with me." Corey stood by the door.

"Corey, stop teasing us," Jack said, flopping down on the pillow again.

"Okay, then," Corey said, pretending to leave the room. "I won't take you to Sans Souci Park with me."

"Sans Souci?" Sammy sat up and rubbed his eyes. "Are you teasin' us, Corey?"

"No, I'm not. See this money?" Corey held up the two bills in his hand. "That's for us to spend at the carnival!"

The boys were instantly awake and already pulling their clothes out of the dresser drawers.

"Don't make noise. Mom is sleeping," Corey ordered. "Be sure to put on your boots. I heard it will rain today and the roads will get muddy. After you're dressed, come down for breakfast, and then we'll be off. If we get there early, we won't have to wait in lines."

Dad waved good-bye at the door as Corey's younger brothers sprinted up the road ahead of him. Corey wanted to see Mom, but Dad said, "Let her sleep."

They walked along the paved road into the town that nestled in the river valley. Jack and Sammy kept running along the railroad tracks by the river. As they got closer to the park, the river lapped over the shore and crossed the main street. Jack and Sammy sloshed around in the water, splashing each other.

"Stop it! Come over here," Corey yelled. "You'll be soaked before we even get to Sans Souci!"

They could hear the music of the calliope become louder as they approached.

A long line of kids and parents wove into the park, slowly, trying to avoid puddles, and not knowing where to go first. Most everyone was dressed up—women in big hats and wearing long skirts that dipped into the puddles and mud. Men and children were in their Sunday-go-to-meeting suits. This was an occasion, and the families loved festivities—even when the weather was threatening.

"There's the carousel!" Sammy yelled, pointing. "I want to ride."

Jack pulled Corey's arm in another direction. "No, let's go over there. If you throw a ring onto those sticks, you win a toy."

Sammy took off for the merry-go-round and Corey had to catch him. When he looked back, Jack was standing by the game booth, watching as a young man tried his luck with the rings.

Soon Corey realized that keeping his brothers together would not be easy. He pulled them aside and laid down the law. "You have to stay with me. If you go off by yourself, we'll turn around and go home," he threatened. "That's the rule. We stick together."

When the boys had settled down, Corey suggested, "Let's walk around and see what's here before we decide on anything."

They sauntered along, stopping occasionally to listen to a barker promote his show or his wares. Corey felt Jack tug at his sleeve. "Look over there." He pointed to a small stage, where the tiniest woman he had ever seen stood. She was as beautiful as a little fairy in her jeweled gown. A golden crown sparkled on her head.

"Step right up, ladies and gentlemen!" shouted another barker. "Come in and see the lovely little princess, who is only twenty-two inches tall but is as perfect a lady as you will ever see!"

"Is she real?" Sammy asked.

"No, she's a doll," Jack whispered.

"She's real. She's just like us—except she's little." Corey pointed to the next booth, where a tall, huge young man strode around on the stage. "Look, there's a giant."

"Holy cow!" Jack whispered.

Sammy stood silently, his mouth open.

The man seemed as tall as a tree, with legs as large as tree trunks. Corey pretended to be unimpressed.

"Will I grow that tall?" Jack asked.

"No, of course not. You would be taller than most kids by now. You're average," Corey told him.

"How big is his house?" Sammy whispered.

"How should I know?" Corey replied. "I have no idea where he lives."

"Maybe that little lady lives in a dollhouse," Sammy suggested.

"There are lots of things to see," Corey said. "Let's move on."

When they approached the carousel, Sammy insisted, "I want to ride!" Corey finally relented and decided he should ride too, to keep a close watch on his brothers. He hated to spend the extra money for himself, since it wouldn't take long to use up the money early in the day. Besides, he saw a ride he wanted to take on the other side of the carnival—the House of Horrors. That sounded exciting and fun, but it might be too scary for the boys. So he bought three tickets to the merry-go-round.

The loud, wheezy music of the calliope drowned out the noise of the crowds as they climbed on the carousel. Jack chose a white charger that was so big that Corey had to have help from a man who was riding with his young son. Together they boosted Jack high onto the saddle atop the white stallion.

Sammy found a fierce-looking tiger and climbed on its back. Corey stood between both of them and held on to a brass pole. Gradually the carousel started turning, and the calliope sang its loud, windy song, "Hello, my baby, hello, my honey, hello, my ragtime gal."

Corey hoped no one from the breaker would see him riding on the merry-go-round. As the carousel whirled faster, Corey became dizzy from watching the world flying by. He was relieved when the ride slowed to a stop and he pulled his brothers off.

Now it was his turn. As he dragged the kids to the House of Horrors, Corey wondered again if the boys might be scared on the spooky ride. Yet if he had to keep paying for three of them, counting himself, they'd run out of money before long.

Then he spotted his neighbors, the Sullivan family, meandering through the carnival. "Mrs. Sullivan!" he called, running up to them.

"Well, hello there, Corey," Mrs. Sullivan said. "How nice that you took your brothers to the park today. It gives your mother a break. Has she had the baby yet?"

"No, but any time now. That's why I brought the boys. I wondered if you would watch them just for a few minutes while I go into the House of Horrors. They might be scared if I take them with me. I really wanted to try it myself."

"Yes, I'll watch them," Mrs. Sullivan said. "We'll stay here until your ride is over."

"Thanks!" He turned to the boys and said, "Mrs. Sullivan will watch you while I take a ride. So be good."

"I want to go too," Jack said.

"No, this is my turn," Corey whispered, hoping the boys wouldn't make a scene. "Just wait for a few minutes." He ran to the ticket booth, bought a ticket, and climbed into the car waiting nearby.

Before Corey could settle himself into the seat, the car began rolling along its tracks and pushed through the double doors.

Corey started his dark journey through the House of Horrors.

31
House of Horrors

At first, everything was black—not a spot of light or color. Corey could feel wind blowing all around, but where did it come from? There were no windows or doors that he could see.

Ahead, glowing in the darkness, a glass coffin appeared with a glaring, white skeleton lying inside. It looked straight at Corey with empty eyes, then sat up abruptly. Corey held his breath as the car headed straight for the coffin. The hair stood up on his arms, as there seemed no way out. Then, suddenly, the car swerved, just missing the coffin by a hairbreadth. The car turned sharply and everything was black again as he rode into another chamber.

This room was filled with flying things that reached down with clammy hands and wings and touched his hair and arms. Whatever they were, they were everywhere. Moans and screams added to the terror.

Then it happened—the very thing for which Corey should have been prepared—he began to sweat and feel sick. It was the same panic he had in the mine and in his dreams—of being powerless, of sinking under a solid roof, from which he could never escape.

He suddenly forgot where he was or what was happening. Where was he? Was he back in the mine? He couldn't tell if he was up or down or in what direction the car was taking him. His throat tightened, and he struggled to breathe.

Corey forced himself to think apart from the overpowering fear. He should have known the ride would send him into a dark, closed-in, cavelike place, like the mines.

Could he get control of the panic that was already making his arms and legs tremble? Or was it too late? He hadn't been prepared for this reaction. *Taking a ride in here was a stupid thing to do!*

"This is only make-believe," he said out loud. "There is not one whit of horror in here at all. It's just a silly ride. Everything is fake. Mrs. Chudzik's house is spookier than this dumb thing."

He had a strong urge to jump out of the car and to run to safety. A pounding headache overpowered the clacking of the wheels as it rattled along the track. Was he back in the coal car racing through the mine with the stone roof tight overhead? Where was he?

Take a breath. Think. He was in the House of Horrors.

He was safe, and there was no danger. "I'm fine. Nothing bad will happen," Corey assured himself over and over as the car flew through the maze of shoddy hallways. "This is a stupid kids' ride. In a minute, I'll be out in the sunshine again."

Corey's words became stronger, and gradually, in the midst of the House of Horrors, with goblins howling and grabbing at him, with flashing lights blinding him, Corey felt the panic slipping away. His breathing became easier, the sweating stopped, and he no longer felt dizzy and sick. And just as the car shot through the last set of double doors into the bright sunlight, the terror was gone.

His brothers were waiting at the barrier gate to the ride, their eyes wide and curious as Corey emerged smiling triumphantly.

32
The Genie's Castle

Corey jumped out of the car and leaped over the guardrail to where his brothers stood nearby with Mrs. Sullivan.

"Are you all right?" Mrs. Sullivan asked. "You seem wound up. Was the ride exciting?"

"Yep, it sure was. Best ride I've ever had," Corey said, grinning. "Thanks for watching the boys. They would have been scared with all the skeletons and goblins."

"Were you scared, Corey?" Jack asked.

"Oh, I was scared, all right," Corey said.

"Aw, I want to go on that ride," Jack begged.

"Me too," Sammy agreed.

"We'll find something else." Corey turned to Mrs. Sullivan. "Thanks again. I needed that ride."

Mrs. Sullivan looked sideways at Corey and raised her eyebrows. "You needed that ride, did you?"

"It's a long story, but yes, I did."

"Give your mother a hug for me," she said, walking away. "I'll be in touch with her soon—after the baby is born."

Corey wondered if the baby would arrive while they were gone.

The three brothers continued on their way around the carnival and soon came to a fun house with the name the Genie's Castle. Corey bought three tickets. The entrance was built to look like a magic lamp with smoke curling up from its chimney. Once inside, the first obstacle was a huge barrel that rotated in full circles.

Sammy, always the daring one, hopped right inside, but as the great cask turned, he fell onto the whirling floor, laughing as he tried to stand. Corey grabbed Jack's hand, and the two of them tried to get through the barrel but kept falling. After a while, the boys moved quickly enough to escape the rotation and enter the first room of the fun house.

Mirrors covered every wall of the large chamber. One mirror stretched Jack out as tall as the giant he'd seen earlier. In the reflection, his legs were as thin as clotheslines. His face and chin were skinny and twice as long. Jack doubled up with laughter and then ran to the other mirrors.

Sammy was worried when he first looked into one of the mirrors and saw himself with a chubby round belly and eyes peering out from a face like a fat balloon. "Will I look like this forever?"

Corey laughed. "No, of course not."

After they'd moved from mirror to mirror and howled at every reflected image, they decided to move on. However, there was no door. Every wall was mounted with mirrors.

Jack was puzzled. "How did we get in, and how do we get out?"

Corey went to each mirror until he finally found the door that led them to a hallway. As they stepped onto the floor, Corey felt the floor jiggle and slant in every direction. The boys could barely stand. But then, as they reached a closed door, *wham!* The entire passageway plunged.

"Coreeeeey!" Jack screamed.

"Help!" Sammy yelled.

When Corey lost his balance and fell to the floor, he thought they had fallen into a chasm. Then he realized the floor had only dropped a few inches. Feeling foolish, Corey picked himself up. "You're both okay. It's a trick floor."

By the time they left the Genie's Castle, it was raining, and they were hungry. Corey asked someone the time, and he realized it was afternoon already. "Let's have our hot dogs now, before we use up any more of our money," Corey suggested. Farther down the walkway, a vendor was selling hot potatoes and *zapiekanki*—kielbasa sandwiches—for only ten cents each. He ordered two, instead of the hot dogs. One he'd cut in half for his brothers.

The boys sat at a red-painted wooden table under an awning and waited until the waiter brought their lunch. When it finally came, the French bread was crusty and loaded with slices of kielbasa, mushrooms, and melted cheese that dripped in strings from the meat. As Corey cut a sandwich in two, he realized how hungry he was.

Corey grabbed extra napkins from the counter and tucked a napkin under each of his brothers' necks.

"No! We don't want bibs, Corey," Jack said, pulling the napkin away.

Corey stuffed another napkin under his brother's chin. "You will need them with all that melted cheese and mushrooms."

"We'll just have water to drink," Corey told the waiter. There were other rides and sights he wanted to see.

As they were eating, Corey heard familiar voices and looked up to see Charlie, Frank, and Paddy heading their way. They wore backpacks, and Corey could see their bats sticking out.

"Well, look who's here," Charlie said. "If you're comin' to play tomorrow, you'll have to try out for the team first, you know."

"When can I try out?" Corey asked.

"Now."

"In the rain?"

"A little rain won't hurt you."

"There's goin' to be flooding, and we have to walk home."

"Maybe those kids over there might want to try out,"

Frank said, pointing to a group of boys hovering near a shed to stay dry. "They work in our breaker."

"Ask them," Paddy said.

Corey recognized three brothers, Ivan, Benes, and Karol. The other two were their cousins, Danin and Tank. They lived with their families in Anthony's patch. They were all breaker boys but seldom mixed with the other kids.

"Do they play ball?" Corey asked. "I've never seen them play."

"Naw. They're not good at bat," Charlie said.

"Have they ever tried out?" Corey inquired.

"We don't let those kids try out. They don't even speak English," Frank said. "How do you explain the game, when they're so stupid they don't understand a word you're saying?"

"They're not stupid just because they don't speak English," Corey said. "I'll bet they understand more than they let on. Do you know how to speak any other language?"

"No, my folks won't let me speak anything but English at home," Charlie said, "even though they do speak German when they don't want me to understand what they're sayin.'"

"Does anyone know those kids, really?" Paddy asked.

"Nope. They're Slavic and they go to that onion church up on the hill. The orthopedic church," Frank said.

"That church with the dome is the Orthodox church, you dummy," Corey said. "And you call *them* stupid?"

"What Frank means is they don't go to our church," Charlie explained. "So we don't know much about them. Even their writing looks weird. They don't use our alphabet."

"What difference if they go to the onion church? What difference if they have a different alphabet?" Corey asked. "They might be great ballplayers."

"Well, I suppose we could give them a try," Charlie said after a moment's thought. "If we want to play for the championship, we need players." He called to one of the boys. "Hey, Ivan! Come here!"

Ivan looked up and around, then, seeing Charlie, he turned away.

"You too, Benny and Karol," Charlie called. "Come over here."

Frank whispered, "How do ya like Karol for a name? It's a girls' name, for Pete's sake."

"Maybe we could call him Karl," Corey suggested.

The five boys across the walkway whispered to one another, then came cautiously over to the picnic area where Corey and the others were waiting.

"Hey, you guys," Frank bellowed. "How would you like to play baseball with us tomorrow? But first you need to try out this afternoon in the park over there." He pointed to the other side of the field where the game was to be held on Sunday.

Benes—whom everyone called Benny—used his hands to talk. "Ball?" he asked Frank, pitching an imaginary ball and then batting it. He seemed to understand what Frank was saying.

"Yeah. Baseball," Charlie yelled.

"They're not deaf," Corey muttered. "Why are you shouting?"

"You . . . kids." Charlie ignored Corey and continued to speak loudly as he pointed to each of the boys. "Now."

The boys talked with one another in their own language, then nodded, and the five Slavic boys went off with Charlie, Frank, and Paddy toward the empty field where the game would be held on Sunday—if the field wasn't flooded by then.

"Are you comin', Corey?" Charlie called. "You haven't tried out yet."

Corey shook his head. "I've got to get the kids home before it starts pouring. I'll try out tomorrow, before the game, if the field isn't flooded."

The clouds were low and black, and by the time the boys headed home, the driving rain had made the walks and the main roads all mud and deep puddles.

Corey thought about how his day at the park had helped him get a new view on his life. He knew it would take more time, but after his adventure in the House of Horrors, he was sure he had the power to conquer his phobia. If he could do it once—like on the ride—then he could do it again, couldn't he? He could get better in time. Who would have thought a carnival ride could do all that?

He was eager to see Mrs. Chudzik and tell her what had happened. *She has a special understanding of things that ordinary people don't have. Perhaps it was her education in*

Europe. It seems like lots of famous, intelligent people come from Europe. That would include Ivan, Benny, and Karol. They may be real smart, if we could only understand what they were saying.

Corey walked home at a fast pace, thinking his own thoughts, hardly noticing he and his brothers were soaked.

"Slow down, Corey," Jack yelled.

"I'm tired," Sammy complained.

"Come on. We may have a new brother or sister," Corey told them. "Don't you want to find out?"

"I don't want a sister," Jack said. "Girls are dumb."

"No, they are not," Corey said.

"Mom is a girl, but she's not dumb," Sammy said. "She's just tired a lot."

It was dark when they reached their patch, and the smell of kerosene lanterns drifted through the neighborhood. As they turned down to their own house, Corey broke into a run. He could hardly wait to hear if the baby had come and to tell Dad and Mom what a good time they had at Sans Souci Park.

Then he stopped abruptly. What was going on at his house? Lights glared from every window—and parked out front was a bright red touring car.

33

Emergency!

Corey reached the front steps ahead of his brothers and stomped up onto the porch. "Mom! Dad!" he yelled as he burst through the door.

Dad met him, his finger to his lips. "Quiet! No noise."

"Is Mom all right?" Corey asked. "Has she had the baby?"

"She's having trouble, Corey. We hoped to get her to a hospital. Mr. Balaski went to the police to get help and an ambulance, but was told the river had flooded and the roads to Scranton were impassible."

"A hospital? Why?" Then Corey had a terrible thought. "Is Mom goin' to—"

"Shh! Corey, don't frighten your brothers," Dad whispered as the boys came into the house. "When I couldn't get any help or doctor, I thought of Mrs. Chudzik. So Mr. Balaski hitched up his horse and took me to her house. She came right away in her auto, but she said the roads were dangerous to go to a hospital anywhere."

For the first time in his life, Corey saw fear in his father's eyes. "What's going to happen?" Corey whispered.

"Mrs. Chudzik examined Mom and said she'd take Mom to her house. She'll keep a close watch, and if Mom needs surgery, she has everything there that they will need."

"What's wrong? Where's Mom?" Sammy pleaded, pulling at Dad's shirt.

"Yeah, what's goin' on?" Jack asked.

"Mrs. Chudzik is going to help Mom," Dad said in a calm voice. "Everything will be all right."

"Do we have a new brother?" Sammy asked.

"Not yet," Dad answered. "But pretty soon." He put his arm on Corey's shoulder. "Corey, take the boys into the kitchen and find something to eat. Then they should go to bed. I'm counting on you to handle things here while I go with Mom to Mrs. Chudzik's."

Mrs. Brady, one of the women who'd come to help, stood nearby shaking her head. "You cannot let that woman take Annie to her house," she said in a loud whisper. "Who knows what will happen to her. You've heard all the stories. . . ."

Corey swung around. "Mrs. Chudzik is a doctor, and she's my friend. Don't say another word against her!"

Mrs. Brady stood back, her mouth open. "Well, I

never. . . ." She scurried into the kitchen, crossing herself and muttering.

Corey turned to his father. "We'll be fine, Dad. Get Mom to Mrs. Chudzik's before the roads get any worse."

"Thanks, son," Dad said, heading to the bedroom where Mom was resting. He came out in a few minutes, cradling Mom in his arms, with Mrs. Chudzik close behind them.

Corey went to his mother and squeezed her hand. "Everything is going to be fine, Mom. Mrs. Chudzik will take good care of you . . . and the baby."

Mom nodded and half smiled as Dad carried her out to the waiting car.

Mrs. Balaski brought over a supper and set it in the still-hot oven. "First, get out of those wet clothes. What were you doing? Swimming in the river?"

"The river was coming up onto the roads and into the park," Corey told her. "Then it poured, too."

The boys went upstairs and got into dry pajamas, then took their wet clothes and brought them down to Mrs. Balaski, who shoved them into a basket.

"Why did Mom go away?" Sammy whispered to Corey. "Is she sick?"

"She's gone to Mrs. Chudzik's to have the baby," Corey said. "She needs help and Mrs. Chudzik knows how to help her."

"Why did Mrs. Brady say those mean things about Mrs. Chudzik?" Jack asked. "Doesn't she like her?"

"Do you like her?" Corey asked, suddenly curious. *Has the neighborhood gossip reached Jack and Sammy yet?*

"Kids say she's bad," Jack said.

"Like the wicked witch in fairy tales," Sammy added. "But I like her."

"Me too," Jack agreed. "She's like having a grandma again."

Mrs. Balaski came into the room. "Have you boys eaten? There's a hot dinner in the oven."

"I don't want to go into the kitchen with Mrs. Brady," Sammy grumbled.

Mrs. Balaski went back to the kitchen. Corey could hear Mrs. Brady's angry voice. "Do you know where they took Annie? They took her to the Chudzik mansion. Can you imagine?"

"Don't get in a lather," Mrs. Balaski said. "Annie was happy and relieved when she saw Mrs. Chudzik come into the room. She said, 'Everything will be all right now.'"

"She must have been feverish."

"You certainly don't believe those stories about Mrs. Chudzik, do you?" Mrs. Balaski asked. "I thought you were an intelligent woman, Colleen."

"Well, I am, but—"

"Mrs. Chudzik is a professional nurse and Annie is in good hands."

Mrs. Balaski took all three boys and her hot casserole to her house. Her husband, who was also a miner, had gone to bed. After a bowl of hunter's stew and homemade bread, Jack and Sammy fell asleep together on the couch in the parlor. Corey, though, squirmed restlessly in an armchair, wondering if his mom was all right and when she'd be home. *Both Mrs. Chudzik and Mom say that women were made to have babies. So everything will be fine, won't it?* he asked himself over and over.

Eventually, the tiring day, the sound of rain tapping against the windows, and the quiet, even breathing of his brothers slowly lured Corey into a deep, dreamless sleep.

34
Making Plans

It was late when Corey woke on Sunday morning and realized where he was. The Balaskis were sleeping. The boys were still curled up together on the sofa. Corey tiptoed to the window, looking to see if there were any signs of his parents at his house, but everything was quiet. The rain was pelting and sweeping in gusts of wind. *The baseball game must have been called off,* Corey decided.

Corey slipped on his shoes and went quietly out of the neighbors' house and across the yard to the back porch of his house. He went into the open back door and into the kitchen, where Dad was seated at the table.

"When did you get back? Did Mom have the baby?"

"No, the baby has decided it's not time yet."

Corey noticed how red and weary Dad's eyes were, and

a shiver of fear passed over him. "How is Mom? Is she all right?"

"Mom will be all right once she has the baby," Dad answered. "Mrs. Chudzik thinks the baby might come by surgery. If that happens, it will be a while before she can be up and around. You see, if she were here alone, there would be no one here to take care of her. You and I will be working—and God knows we need the money more than ever."

"So where's Mom now?" Corey asked.

"Mrs. Chudzik is keeping Mom at her house until she has the baby and is well enough to come home. That lady has turned out to be a godsend, Corey." Dad rested his head in his hands. "I don't know what might have happened if Mrs. Chudzik hadn't come over and taken Mom to her house. She was a baby doctor in Poland. She knows all about having babies."

Corey sat at the table across from his father. "Jack and Sammy had a good time with me yesterday at the park. We'll be fine, so why don't you go back to Mrs. Chudzik's to stay with Mom."

Dad folded his hands. "Here's the plan. I will stay with Mom at Mrs. Chudzik's tonight—maybe even longer, depending on whether Mom needs surgery. A *Cesarean*, they call it. Mrs. Balaski will see the boys off to school in the mornings, and she'll keep an eye on them after school until you get home." Dad got up, poured two cups of coffee, and handed one to Corey. "You'll need this," Dad said, sitting down again. He faced Corey with grave eyes.

"You're only twelve, son, but we're counting on you."

"I know, Dad."

"I've got to open up that new vein of anthracite at the North Star working. It's deep in the mine—almost a half mile or so back from the gangway. I've been busy shoring up the roof, but the bosses are badgering me to get the chamber working." He took a sip of coffee. "I'd like you to go to the mine boss early tomorrow to see if I've signed in. I may be working tomorrow when you get there," Dad said. "But if I'm not, the boss will want to know why I'm not at work on North Star. Then you need to tell him that I'm with Mom and that I'll start blasting the new vein on Tuesday. It's only one day later. It would be too dangerous for me to use dynamite tomorrow, when I'm tired. Besides, the roof of that North Star needs more support. I'm not sure it would hold up if I dynamite. Another day will give Ken a chance to reinforce the ceiling. So it won't be a wasted day. But I sure hope the boss will get more timbers for Ken to use."

"I'll go first thing in the morning before I go to work to explain everything, if you're not there. I wish we had a telephone. It would save a lot of time, wouldn't it?"

"Someday, I suppose, everyone will have a telephone," Dad said.

"Go back and be with Mom," Corey said. "Everything will be fine here."

35
North Star Shaft

Corey was a little late when he arrived at the colliery. First thing he did was to head for the office to see Mr. McBride.

Mr. McBride was sitting at his desk when Corey walked in. "Hey, Corey, where's your dad? He hasn't signed in yet. I thought he was going to start blasting today."

"He was going to start today, sir, but they thought my mom would be having a baby and it was a long night. In fact, she may need surgery. Since he had no sleep, he doesn't think it's a good time for him to use dynamite. He said he'll start blasting tomorrow. But in the meantime, he hoped the timbers would be delivered so his butty Ken could shore up that ceiling. They've been waiting on more lumber for over a week. So if you can get the lumber down there today, it won't be a wasted day. It would be safer if the walls and ceiling of North Star were more stable than they are."

"Today?" Mr. McBride raised an eyebrow. "He wants the timber today? Since when do the miners give the orders—let alone their kids?" He shook his head. "Listen, Corey. How can I tell the big bosses up at the office that we're not blasting? See how it makes me look? They want that new vein opened and working right away."

"Even if it's dangerous?" Corey asked. "Even if the roof is unstable? And who's to blame for not delivering the timbers?"

Mr. McBride ignored the question as he twiddled his thumbs. "The bosses won't be happy." Then he straightened up and noticed Corey again. "You go down the North Star shaft—and tell Mr. Farley and Ken that they'll be blasting tomorrow instead." Mr. McBride suddenly pointed his finger at Corey. "Wait a minute. I can't let you go down into the mine. You had a bad time that day I took you down in the coal car. You nearly killed yourself."

"I'm better now," Corey protested. He had hoped Mr. McBride had forgotten that day. "I'm pretty sure I'll be okay."

"Pretty sure?" Mr. McBride burst out. "You can't be pretty sure down in the mine."

"I'll be fine," Corey stated as he headed for the door. "Just tell me the way, that's all."

"Well, go ahead, then, if you're so certain." Mr. McBride led him to the elevator cage that went down the shaft into the mine, and opened the cage door for Corey.

"The fire boss's office is . . . where?" Corey asked.

"You'll see it when you get there," Mr. McBride called as the cage descended. "You can't miss it. It's a whitewashed hole-in-the-wall."

For a moment, Corey watched the rocky walls slip by as he dropped deeper and deeper into the mine. He began to feel dizzy but tried to ignore it. By the time the cage came to a clattery stop, it was cold and the air smelled dank. He stepped out onto the uneven ground, just as someone above hoisted the cage back to the surface.

As the elevator disappeared from sight, Corey felt he was trapped in the giant hole. Panic crept into his body, like a chill. *I can't let this get to me*, he told himself as he looked around for the white room.

Then he saw the room. It was just as Mr. McBride said—a whitewashed room, carved into the rocky wall. It stood out bright in the darkness, reminding him of the first aid room. *That must be the fire boss's office*, Corey decided, and headed for it.

Inside the little chamber, a map of the underground tunnels of the mine lay open on a small desk. On the wall hung a pegboard with brass tags with numbers on them. Dad had told him how it worked. Miners put their tags on the pegboard every morning, once they knew where they would be working in the mine. Then, if a tag was still on the pegboard at closing time, the boss knew something could be wrong and who might be in danger and where.

"Hey, aren't you Joe Adamski's son?" a voice boomed.

Corey looked up to see a thin man wearing a carbide lantern on his belt.

"Yes, I'm Corey."

"I'm Sean Farley, the fire boss. What are you doin' here? Where's your father?"

"I'm here for my dad. He wanted me to tell you and Ken Keenan that he won't be in today or be blasting that new vein of coal until tomorrow."

Mr. Farley frowned. "Not blasting? How come?"

Corey explained that his father was extremely tired and what had happened with his mother. "Dad said they could use another day to shore up the ceiling, but the lumber hasn't been delivered yet." Then he asked, "Will you inform Ken Keenan, Dad's butty?"

"No, I'll leave that up to you. I'm not a messenger boy."

I'll have to go down to the North Star, Corey realized. *Will I be able to go all that way without having a spell?*

"Will you show me how to get to the North Star?" he asked.

"This here's a map of the workings." The fire boss pointed to the map on his desk. "You can read a map, can't you?"

Corey didn't want to make Mr. Farley any angrier than he was. "Yes, sir," he said as he studied the map. Dad had told him many times how the gangways went through the mine, like avenues. The working sites were situated off them like streets. Dad was in the new one at the very end. Corey traced the map with his finger until he found an *X* at the end of the main gangway, and the name "North Star" scribbled on the map.

As Corey headed down the gangway, he repeated in his mind, *I'm safe. Nothing can hurt me. I've come all this way into the mine, and nothing bad has happened to me.*

He came to a boy sitting on a stool, next to a large wooden door. The boy jumped up when he saw Corey and hurried to open the door for him.

"I'm heading to the North Star, where my dad works," Corey explained.

"I figured you didn't work here," the boy said, holding the heavy door.

"I work on the breaker," Corey told him. "Do you like your job as a nipper?"

The boy shrugged. "It's all right, I guess."

"Why do they have doors between the sections of the mine?"

"These heavy doors keep poisonous gases from leaking into other chambers. Fresh air is pumped down through pipes and ventilation shafts. We don't want poison gas to mix with the good air."

Dad had already told Corey this information many times, but hearing the boy talk kept Corey's mind off the mine itself.

The nipper held the door open. "It's my job to pay attention and listen for the sound of cars, loaded with tons of coal, barreling down the tracks. We have to move fast and get those doors open in time—or else there's a crash, and a whale of a mess. In fact, I have to get out of the way once the doors are open or else I'd be nothin' but mincemeat."

Corey winced at the word "mincemeat." "Do they always come fast—the coal cars, I mean?"

"Not if a spragger can stop them in time. Or if a mule is bringin' coal cars and there's no incline. One mule can bring four cars."

"That seems heavy for one mule," Corey said as he went through the open door.

"Mules are strong. They don't mind bringing four—but if you try to trick them by sneaking an extra car on, they'll stop and not move. You can't fool a mule." The boy shut the door behind Corey with a loud *clank*.

Once again, Corey felt as if the world outside was shut away from him, but this time he did not feel the old panic rise up. He had a job to do, and that thought seemed to guard him from the fear.

Once he was in even deeper, Corey noticed some of the chambers off the main gangway had names posted over them. BEAR'S CAVE; ROCKY RUN; HOLE-IN-THE-WALL.

He saw a narrower tunnel that headed in another direction with the name East Wind. If that chamber went toward the east, then he must be turning north now. Too bad all the chambers didn't have a direction in their names.

He tromped down the rocky road through the gloomy walls of stone. Corey thought about the world above, which had the sky for its roof—a blue sky with flying clouds that turned golden at sunset. *No wonder Dad never wanted us to end up in the mines.* Except for a few hours a week with his family, Dad spent his life cooped up inside the mine and its dark, stone tunnels. Would that be Corey's future too?

The walkways were getting rougher and dark when he reached a branch off to the right and saw the sign for North Star. A dark opening, like the jaw of a dragon, opened deep into the center of the mountain. Dad would be blasting in there somewhere tomorrow. Massive timbers had been jammed into the ceiling and walls to brace them.

Ken appeared from the darkness of the new tunnel, his carbide lamp lighting his face and the area around him. "Hey, Corey, what a surprise! Look at you, down here in the mine!"

Dad must have told Ken about that day I passed out. Corey felt his face flush with embarrassment. *How many others did he tell?*

"Dad wanted you to know he wouldn't be in today to start blasting," Corey told him. "Mom had a hard time last night, thinking she'd have the baby. But she didn't. Today the doctor may be doing an operation."

"Oh, so Annie may have that Cesarean operation they talk about? I hope she has a good doctor," said Ken.

"The best," Corey answered. "Dad was up all night, so he thought it would be better to wait on the blasting until tomorrow." He looked around. "You have timbers here propping up the ceiling, don't you?"

"Yeah—but inside the new shaft, the ceiling is unstable and unpredictable. We need to prop that roof up more before we start blasting anyway. I'm still waiting for the timber. What's the matter with the bosses? I suspect they're worried about the cost. If this roof comes tumblin' down, it'll be their fault, not ours, and *our lives, not theirs.*" Ken stopped, as if remembering Corey's fears.

"How far into the earth does that vein of anthracite go?" Corey asked.

"Do you want to take a look?" Ken asked, beckoning Corey into the darkness.

Corey was determined not to show any fear. Too many folks seemed to know about his phobia. "Sure." He followed Ken deeper into the shaft, bending to keep his head from hitting the low roof, which was just over their heads.

"See this dark streak?" Ken said, pointing to the streak of black stone that wound its way through the shaft. "There's the seam of black diamonds."

"How far does it go?"

"Who knows?" Ken answered. "Maybe to another mountain somewhere."

"I feel like the river must be nearby," Corey said.

"We're not far from the river—especially the deeper we go into the chamber here. If your dad sees any signs of dripping water, we shouldn't blast either. We've had a lot of rain this weekend, and with the flooding down in the town, and the river so high, we'd be in real trouble if the river came in. It would flood the *entire* mine."

Corey stopped as he imagined himself in the narrow shaft, filling fast with river water. His heart beat faster and harder, and sweat broke out on his forehead. "I've got to go to work," he said to Ken. "I'm late." He backed up and then scurried toward the main gangway.

36

Richie and His Mule

Corey had to get away from the darkness of the narrow tunnel near the end of North Star, which seemed to close in on him. Why had the panic come upon him so suddenly?

It was Ken talking about the mine flooding, Corey realized. *The very thought of water filling in the chasms and gangways, with men drowning and struggling to get out . . .*

Corey began to run, and it wasn't until he came to the gangway and the vast chamber with its high ceilings that he slowed to a fast walk.

Then he heard loud singing. It was his old schoolmate Richie Lee, who had left school in fifth grade to become a mule driver. He was riding on his mule, and pulling a coal car, all the while singing at the top of his lungs:

"My sweetheart's the mule in the mines.
I drive her without reins or lines.
On the bumper I sit, where I chew and I spit,
All over my sweetheart's behind."

As Richie came closer, he pulled his mule to a stop. "Hey, Corey!" he called. His mule was covered with leather straps and riggings, and a safety lamp swung from the front of her harness. She paused and tilted her head when she saw Corey.

"Will ya look at that," Richie said. "She thinks she knows you, Corey."

Corey reached out and petted the mule's velvety nose.

"Whatcha doin' down here in the mine?" Richie asked.

"Delivering a message for my dad." He tried to look calm, but his mouth was dry. "Uh, what do you call your mule?"

"I named her Tootsie—like in the song. She's a happy mule 'cause she knows I love her. Don't you, sweetheart?" Richie reached down and patted her neck. Then he tipped his hat and waved to Corey as he rode off.

Tootsie switched her tail and her ears flicked as Richie, who was not a bit shy or self-conscious, continued singing the latest song loudly as he rode away.

"Toot, toot, Tootsie, good-bye,
Toot, toot, Tootsie, don't cry
The choo-choo train that takes me,

Away from you—no words can say how sad it makes me. . . ."

Corey raced again for the elevator. He knew it would take some time yet before he would feel at ease down here in the mine.

"I'm okay," he told himself. "Nothing has happened. Everything in here is safe." But it didn't work. Just when he was thinking he could handle it, the panic took hold.

He found the elevator and tugged at the cord. "Get me up, quick!" he yelled.

37
Spring Training

When Corey finally calmed down and got to work, the boys were already in their seats as the conveyor noisily carried the coal and the rocks down for separating. "You're late, kid!" the supervisor yelled when he saw Corey. He snapped the stick he carried around.

Corey said nothing as he climbed into his usual seat. He noticed his hands were shaking. He looked around to see if Charlie was watching him. There he was near the top of the machine, along with his sidekicks Frank and Paddy. But at least they didn't pay any attention to Corey the rest of the morning.

Only when the whistle blew at noon did Corey realize he had no lunch. He washed his hands, then went outside. It felt like spring today in the warm sun, with birds chirping loudly. Corey could see a few hopeful buds on the branches of trees and could hardly wait for them to burst open into the bright green shades of springtime.

He was disappointed in himself. He'd done so well in the mine until he'd gotten deeper into the North Star. Then he'd gone backward, just when he was sure he was winning over the panic and fear.

Corey looked around for Anthony but didn't see him. Perhaps Anthony was using his lunch hour to check out the spragger job that would be available soon. Except for Anthony, Corey didn't have any real friends. There were dozens of breaker boys, but the only ones he knew were the tough ones like Charlie. The other boys—like the Slavic boys—were quiet and hardworking and hardly ever mixed with the other kids. It looked like Ivan and his friends had already tried out at the park the other day and made the team. They were throwing a baseball back and forth farther out on the field.

Corey sat on a bench nearby and watched Charlie pitch balls, while the boys took turns with the bat. Corey wanted to play on the team—he'd thought he had made that clear. But no one asked him to try out again. If he could stand up there and hit the ball, he'd pretend it was the dark fears inside and smash it right out of sight.

He watched the kids at practice, and slowly he relaxed. He loved to play ball, and he knew spring training would start soon. Once he was focused on baseball, he'd get his mind off his worries and concern for Mom.

Well, I'll never get on the team if I don't speak up for myself, Corey decided. He went over to home base. "Hey, how about giving me a chance to hit the ball?" he asked Frank.

The boys stopped playing for a moment. Then Frank shrugged his shoulders and handed Corey the bat. "Go ahead."

Corey went to the base and swung the bat a few times. Charlie stood waiting, then—*WHOOSH!* He pitched the ball suddenly, and it whizzed right past Corey's head.

"Strike!" Frank shouted.

Before Corey could argue that it was a ball, not a strike, *WHOOSH!* Charlie pitched another ball that Corey never saw.

"Strike two!" Frank shouted, trying not to laugh.

Corey ignored them and took his stance. Charlie pitched again, and this time Corey took a swing and hit the ball off into the field and out of sight.

"Lucky swing," Frank said, shoving Corey away from the base.

"Wait a minute," Charlie called. "Let's try another."

Corey stood with his legs apart, bat ready this time. *WHOOSH!* came the ball.

BAM! Once again, Corey hit the ball far into the outfield.

Charlie swaggered in to home base. "Okay," he said, putting an arm around Corey's shoulders. "So you hit a couple of good ones. We might be able to train you." He spit on the ground. "I've decided you can be on the team, if you want."

Corey didn't trust Charlie or Frank, but he sure wanted to be on the team. "Yeah, I'd like to join."

"Whadda ya think, Frank?" Charlie asked. "Have we got some talent here?"

"Maybe, with some trainin'," Frank answered.

Corey saw Charlie wink at Frank and anger welled up inside him. "I saw you wink. Listen, you guys, I'd like to play on this team, and you need a good hitter. But since you can't stop your stupid shenanigans and settle down to play baseball, I'm out of here!" He hurled the bat to the ground and stomped off.

After a moment, Charlie ran after him, grabbed the back of Corey's jacket. "Okay, kid, you're on the team." He turned around to the other boys, who had been waiting around to play. "Let's play ball!"

The breaker boys lined up, and the Mountain Crest baseball team began spring training.

38

Visiting Mom

After work that day, Corey was heading home, when Anthony called to him. "Corey! Wait up!"

"Where were you today?" Corey asked as Anthony caught up with him.

"I helped out down in the mine."

"You missed out. The breaker boys started spring training," Corey told him. "I got on the team."

Anthony stopped walking. "You did? Charlie let you?"

"I hit a few balls into the outfield," Corey told him. "But I told Charlie I'd play only if they'd quit their monkey-shines and play ball."

Anthony laughed. "You told Charlie that? And he didn't beat you up?"

"Nope. He said I made the team. Why don't you try out for the team too?"

"I will," Anthony promised. They passed by Corey's street. "Aren't you goin' home?"

"No, I'm going to Mrs. Chudzik's. My mother is staying with her."

"At Mrs. Chudzik's house?" Anthony's eyes widened and his jaw dropped. "Really?"

"Yes, really," Corey answered. "Mom is staying there until she has the baby. If she needs help, Mrs. Chudzik will be there to help her."

Neither of the boys spoke until they reached Anthony's patch. "Why don't you come with me? You're not afraid, are you?"

"No, course not. Just want to go home," Anthony said, avoiding Corey's eyes. "I'll try out for the team tomorrow."

Corey continued on his way, taking Abby's path. He was eager to see his mother, but he *needed* to see Mrs. Chudzik. He needed to tell her what had happened today at the mine.

His pace quickened as he approached the big house. He took the porch steps two at a time and knocked on the door. Hovi announced Corey's arrival, barking and pacing.

The door opened and Mrs. Chudzik peered out. "Corey, your mother hoped you'd come by after work." She stood back and Corey went inside.

Hovi danced around Corey as he entered. "Yes, it's me, Hovi," Corey exclaimed.

"Annie is out on the porch getting some fresh air," Mrs. Chudzik said, motioning him to the kitchen. "It's sunny out there this time of day."

The back door was open, and the sunlight drifted into the dark kitchen. He tiptoed out onto the porch, hoping his mother was awake. She was nestled in a rocking chair and bundled in a huge, soft quilt that looked brand-new. Only her head was visible as she rocked gently.

"Oh, Corey!" she exclaimed, straightening up in the chair. She pulled her arm out from the blanket and motioned for him to come closer. "I've missed you! I'm so glad you came by." She laughed as Hovi trotted ahead of Corey and lay at her feet.

Corey realized that he hadn't heard Mom laugh in a long time.

She opened her arms and he went to her, kissing her cheek. "I've missed you too, Mom. And so do Jack and Sammy. Dad said you might need surgery."

"We're waiting one more day to see if the baby will come on his own. If not, Mrs. Chudzik will do a Cesarean operation. I trust her completely, Corey." She smiled and patted Corey's hand as if she knew he might be worried. "Now tell me how you and your brothers are doing. How are your brothers? I wish I could see them."

"We're all fine. Mrs. Balaski is watching the boys after school until I get home." Corey sat on a nearby chair and told her about his day at Sans Souci, and how he'd made the baseball team.

He heard a squeaky sound and looked up to see Mrs.

Chudzik wheeling a wooden tea cart, set with a teapot, cups, and a huge plate of sandwiches.

"The wheels need oiling," she said apologetically. "I haven't used it since Dr. Chudzik passed away."

"Just look at how Mrs. Chudzik spoils me." Mom laughed. "I may just stay right here forever!"

Corey's mouth dropped open at Mom's lightheartedness. Mrs. Chudzik must have performed magic to make his tired, sad mother seem so cheerful—even with the scare she'd had the other night and the possibility of surgery tomorrow.

"Won't you please join us, Mrs. Chudzik?" Mom pleaded. Mrs. Chudzik nodded, and Corey pulled another chair closer. They all snacked and chatted in the late-afternoon sunshine.

But Corey needed to talk to Mrs. Chudzik alone. Mrs. Chudzik was *his* friend, and now he couldn't tell Mrs. Chudzik what had happened to him again in the mine, or ask what he should do. Not now, with Mom close by.

39
Disaster!

By the time the whistle blew on Tuesday morning, Corey had already fed his brothers and sent them off to school. He'd made coffee and fixed breakfast and lunch for himself and his father, and they'd gone off to the breaker well ahead of the usual line of workers. When they reached the mine, Dad said, "Thanks for your help, son. It's been tough without your mother. I wish she weren't staying with Mrs. Chudzik. That's made things harder for the rest of us, and the baby isn't even born yet."

"Mrs. Chudzik said she needs rest," Corey reminded him. "Mom was cheerful yesterday, when I saw her. It's been good for her to stay with Mrs. Chudzik."

"Well, I'm glad *she's* cheerful," Dad said. "I wish I

were cheerful. I have a lot of worries on my mind. I'm hoping they sent some strong timbers for Ken to prop up that mine's ceilings. That's the main thing I'm worried about now—if I should blast."

"Don't blast if you think it's not safe, Dad," Corey called as his father went toward the elevator. "Dad?" Corey waited for a response, but Dad didn't answer.

When Corey took his seat at the conveyor, Charlie, who'd proclaimed himself coach of the team, made an announcement from his place at the top of the breaker. "We're havin' ball practice this comin' weekend. Remember, Saturday— at nine a.m. If you're late or not there, you won't be on the team. We want to beat every other club in the valley this year, and we need kids who want to win!"

A cheer went up and Charlie took his seat.

The boss gave the signal, and the breaker began its noisy thrust of sending down the dirty coal.

Corey began sorting the coal and slate in his bins. He worried about the panic attack he'd almost had at the mine yesterday, and he wished he could talk to Mrs. Chudzik without Mom hearing. He decided to think about ball practice instead. He'd show the team what a good hitter he was, and how fast he could run. Concentrating on baseball made the time go by faster, yet he was startled to hear the steam whistle blow. Was it lunchtime already?

The whistle blew—loud, clear, three times, four times. On and on it sounded. An emergency in the mines!

The boys on the breaker froze. Every one of them had a father or brother working in the mine that day.

The breaker stopped. For several moments no one spoke or cried out. Then the boys began talking all at once. "What happened? Where? How bad?" Then, as if given a signal, they jumped up from their seats and raced to the door as the whistle sounded again.

"Stop!" yelled the boss. "I didn't tell you to leave!" Then, knowing the boys were not listening, he shrugged and threw his hands up.

The whistle sounded again as Corey took the stairs down two by two and then struggled to join the crowd who pushed their way through the door. The breaker boys and the boss were storming their way to the mine, and Corey let the mob carry him along.

The boys raced to the engine house, where everyone gathered, making it difficult to get inside or to hear what was being said. "Let me through," Corey demanded, ramming his way through the crowd. "My dad is in the mine."

"It's a roof fall," a miner said. "Down in that new working—the North Star."

Corey's legs went weak when he heard those words— North Star. "Let me in," he yelled again.

"It's Corey Adamski, Joe's son. He needs to know about his dad." It was his friend Richie, the mule driver. "Let him in."

The crowd opened, letting Corey into the engine house. He saw Mr. McBride and called to him. "Where's my dad, Mr. McBride? Is he all right?"

Mr. McBride looked up. When he saw Corey, his brows furrowed. "Corey, come here, son."

Corey stumbled forward, forcing himself to concentrate on what Mr. McBride was about to tell him.

"Corey, my lad, I'm sorry to tell you this. There's been a roof fall. Your dad had just blasted the back wall of the chamber. The timber props couldn't hold the load of the mountain above them, and they failed. He was alone in there. Ken wasn't with him at the time. We're discussing possible ways to get him out." He patted Corey's shoulder and pushed a chair under him.

Corey's eyes were filling rapidly with tears as he sank into the chair. "Is he alive?" Corey could hardly ask the question.

"We don't know, son. We're getting a rescue group together to see what happened. If your dad is inside that chamber, he may be just fine. But then again . . ." Mr. McBride looked up at the other men standing nearby.

"What about black damp?" Corey asked.

"We're checking for gas in the area of the fall," one of the men answered. "But we can't check for it where your father was working. It's jammed up with rocks."

Mr. McBride said quickly, "We'll get air in to your dad as soon as possible."

Corey stood up and yelled, "As soon as possible? Do it NOW." He glared at the men around him. "We all know what the chances are for him to live or breathe if black damp is in there!" Corey grabbed Mr. McBride by the sleeve. "Get air in to him now! That's the first thing you should have done!"

Mr. McBride looked away. "We're hoping for good news, but the roof fall is large. It closed in the gangway that goes into the North Star working. Tons and tons of rock and coal have blocked off that area. It's practically impossible to get ventilation in there."

"Then how can you get air in there to him?" Corey asked.

"First we need to open or dig a shaft of some kind."

"You've got to do *something*."

"Yes, Corey. We'll be working on it, as soon as we're sure the roof is stable in that area of the mine."

"I want to go down there. I want to see the roof fall for myself," Corey said.

"Until we're sure it's safe from further collapse, no one can go down there," Mr. McBride said. "Your mom wouldn't want to lose you, too."

"My dad is not dead!" Then Corey asked, "Is the gangway the only way to the North Star?"

Mr. McBride nodded. "It is, Corey."

"Mr. McBride, I've heard of trapped miners making their way out through a nearby mine or shaft. There's an old mine just up the road. Could it be a way to get him out?" Corey suggested.

"That's good to know, Corey. I'll bring it up at the meeting."

"What meeting?"

"The managers and directors are meeting soon to discuss how to get to your father," Mr. McBride said. "And also to decide what caused the fall. You said your dad was tired and didn't want to blast yesterday."

"That was yesterday. Dad was rested today. He wouldn't have blasted if he wasn't able. But they were waiting for the timbers to prop the roof. Did you see to it that the roof was propped? Were the timbers delivered?"

Ken Keenan, in the back of the room, spoke up. "No, they didn't deliver the timbers," he yelled. "But you guys said Joe and I would be fired if we didn't blast today. It's your fault this happened. Don't shift the blame onto Joe."

The crowd of miners became angry. "Yeah, put the blame on those who deserve it!"

"The mine barons didn't want to spend more money on timber," someone yelled.

Mr. McBride called for order. "We're going to figure out what happened at the meeting."

"The old mine is real close to this one. And there are shafts there—Abby Russell fell into one of them. Don't you see? That old mine might be a way to get to Dad!" Corey said, hoping Mr. McBride even heard him.

"Yes, yes. I'll tell the directors about that possibility," Mr. McBride said, hardly listening. "We're trying to find the safest and most economical way to reach your father." Mr. McBride headed out the door. "Just stay here and I'll let you know what we've decided as soon as the meeting is over."

Corey's mind had already tuned off Mr. McBride's prattle. He wouldn't sit and wait. No, he was sure there was another way to get to his father. All he had to do was find it.

40
Preparations

As Corey left the engine room, he heard someone say, "At least there's only one miner in that cave-in. We can be thankful for that."

Corey turned and shouted, "Well, you can be thankful it's not *your* father down there!" He ran out the door and into the large area where the boys played ball. As he ran, his thoughts came in spurts. He needed to get into that old mine. He couldn't go in through the big cavern in the cliff that had had a roof fall years ago. There was no way he could get through to the mine that way. There might be other long-forgotten exits in the mountain, but where? There was no time to spare. If he could get down into the old mine, he'd look around and see if there was a way into the North Star Chamber.

I can't ask Mrs. Chudzik for help. She wouldn't let me go down into the mine. In fact, she might already have the mine sealed. I hope not. I'll stop by home and get Dad's other Davy light and a pick.

He looked up to see Richie on his mule, trotting toward him. As he came closer, he asked, "Hey, Corey—aren't you going to stick around to find out how your dad is?"

"I have to find a way to help him."

"What can you do by yourself?" Richie asked.

"I can go down into the old mine and see if there's a way to get to Dad from there."

"You mean that old mine down near Abby Russell's house?"

"Yeah, that's the one. I'm sure that the North Star Chamber is close to that old mine. Maybe it's close enough to break through and get my dad out."

"Did you tell the boss that? Wouldn't they give it a try?"

"Mr. McBride wasn't interested in what I had to say. He was going to have a meeting to discuss who was to blame for the roof fall. There's not enough time for a discussion on that. I want to save my dad."

"Get on Tootsie with me, Corey. We can get wherever you need to go faster if we let Tootsie take us."

He reached his hand out and Corey grabbed hold as Richie pulled him up. He swung his leg over the other side of the mule and then held on to Richie's waist.

"Now, where are we going?" Richie asked.

"To my house—to get a Davy light."

"I have two on my mule," Richie said. "That's enough for the two of us."

"What about miner's picks? We might have to pick our way through the old mine."

"I got those, too," Richie said.

"Then let's go," Corey said.

Richie clicked the mule and called, "Giddyup, Tootsie." Corey hung on to Richie as Tootsie galloped lickety-split ahead. Dust and stones spit up from her hooves as the mule raced down the dirt road.

They'd just rounded the bend when they spotted Abby and Anthony running toward home. "Hey!" Richie yelled to them. "Get out of the way!"

"Where are you going?" Anthony hollered as he pulled Abby to the side of the road.

"Can't talk now!" Corey called out as they flew by. "I've got to save my dad!"

They flew over the dirt road, sending up billows of dust. The clouds overhead scattered as if in a frenzy across the sky. It was as if the whistle at the mine had signaled a state of panic in the universe itself.

As he saw the turnoff to his own house, he thought about his brothers and hoped Mrs. Balaski was watching for them. No time to stop. She must have heard the steam whistle echo over the valley and be wondering what was happening.

They passed the Old Shaft Patch Village, where Anthony lived, and soon they were at Abby's shortcut. "Turn here," Corey told Richie.

"Gee!" Richie yelled to Tootsie, who turned right onto the path to Mrs. Chudzik's.

Corey looked up at the hill and could see the black chasm in the cliff. It was not sealed off yet.

Tootsie made her way delicately up the hill over the rocky path. Once the turrets of Mrs. Chudzik's house were visible, Corey's heart leaped. He wished he could tell Mrs. Chudzik where he was going—and to stop the men from sealing the pipe, if they were coming today. But there was no time.

As they came to the end of the trail, Richie pulled Tootsie to a stop. "Now what?" he asked.

Corey could see the red automobile parked in the driveway. Of course she was home. She wouldn't go anywhere with Mom ready to have the baby. Had Mom heard that Dad was trapped in the mine? Would knowing this affect her health or the baby's? He needed to talk with Mrs. Chudzik. But this was the one time he couldn't confide in her, yet this was the time when he needed her the most.

"Where are we goin', Corey?" Richie asked.

"Up to the top of the cliff," Corey answered, pointing to the steep pathway.

41

Inside the Mountain

At the top of the hill, Corey pulled away the rock that covered the pipe. "Here's the only way I know that we can get into the mine."

"It's narrow," Richie said. "It's a wonder Abby didn't fall all the way, she's so tiny. But we'll have to work our way down."

"I think men could get down through there," Corey said.

"Not fat men," Richie said with a laugh. "I'll get those picks off Tootsie's harness now."

He went to Tootsie, whom he had tied to a tree, then he whispered, "Listen! Someone's coming."

"Who could it be?" Corey said in a low voice.

"It's Abby and me." Anthony appeared from among the trees. "What can we do to help?"

"I knew you might be trying to get down into this mine, so I went home and took the new map of the mine from Papa's desk," Abby said. "And I brought a compass."

"I stopped by my house and got a pick and a spade in case they were needed." Anthony held them up.

Corey almost threw his arms around both of them. "Yes, you can help. Abby, you can stay up here and keep watch. We need someone to stay close to the pipe, so we can call for help if we need it."

Richie unhitched the picks from Tootsie and gave them to Corey. "We can take the handles off so it will be easier for us to carry them down the pipe."

The three boys looked at one another. "So, are we ready?" Corey asked. "I'm going first, because it's my dad who's trapped down there."

"You don't know for sure if he's trapped inside this mine," Richie reminded him.

"I know, but if I don't try, I'll never forgive myself if we find later that he is in there." He sat on the edge of the pipe and was about to drop, when he stopped. "Richie, you know how to read the carbide lights. So you should go first and see if there's any bad gas."

"I have an idea," Abby said. She went to Tootsie and pulled a rope that was coiled up on Tootsie's harness. She tossed one end of the rope to Richie. "Tie it around your waist. Tug on this line if there's any sign of gas and we'll pull you up, Richie."

"I'm ready." He held the small miner's pick close to his chest as he dropped down into the pipe.

"If the lamp dims or acts differently, there is gas in the vicinity; you need to get out immediately," Abby reminded him.

Richie dropped into the rusty pipe. After a few minutes, he called out, "I'm at the bottom and I'm checking for gas on the walls and ceiling with my lamp." Corey and Anthony stayed by the pipe, listening.

"It's safe!" Richie called. "Pull up the rope and let the next one down."

Corey looked into the pipe. "What do you see down there?" he yelled.

"There's a path here at the bottom of the pipe that goes to the right or the left."

"We want to go to the right," Corey called as he checked the map. "That's the direction of the old gangway." He examined the map more closely. "I wonder what those two circles mean. There are only two, and one seems to show this pipe."

Abby handed the rope to Corey, who hitched it around his waist. After he took the pick, he said a silent prayer and lowered himself.

The trip down was sudden and swift, but in spots, Corey, who was a little stockier than Richie, had to work himself through places where the pipe narrowed, or his pants or jacket caught on rough pieces of pipe and he had to pull himself free.

Anthony came down quickly and easily. The boys aimed their lights at the narrow passageway with its walls of stone. The pathway went in two directions, as Richie had said.

Corey was extremely mindful that he was in a narrow tunnel with stone walls around him—like a grave. Beads of sweat were already dripping down his face. He took a deep breath and smelled the scent of musty, dead air. *I will not let this mine keep me from my dad. I am alive and well, and I'm going to find him.*

The three boys, armed with the mining tools, made their way down the passage, with Richie in the lead, heading toward the old mine.

"Are you all right?" Abby's concerned voice called from far away.

"We're okay!" Corey yelled, hoping she could hear him.

Abby answered, but he could not make out what she said.

As they moved along slowly, Corey warned, "Watch out for holes, Richie. There could be chasms that drop hundreds of feet."

"There sure are lots of dangers in here," Anthony whispered in a jittery voice.

The old familiar feeling of panic was taking hold of Corey. His head ached, and he felt as if the stone walls were squeezing in on him. But there was no time to think about it. This was a *feeling*, not anything real. He pushed the feelings out of his thoughts.

The stone path sloped downward, deep into the mountain. It was becoming rougher—obviously less used and less traveled in the past. Their carbide lights made eerie shadows on the rocky surface of the walls and roof.

Suddenly, just when they were beginning to feel the

tunnel was endless, they came to an opening—a yawning, gaping cavern.

"We're inside the mine," Richie yelled. "This must be the gangway. Wait until I check for gas." He headed into the vast, cavernous opening, testing the air in the chamber. He held his lamp to the ground, the walls, and as far as he could reach to the ceiling. "It's safe!"

Corey stepped out into what seemed to be the main chamber of the mine. The boys stood silently as they glanced around. The old timbers that supported the roof were black with mold. Some were bent like broken legs, and Corey knew that meant the mountain was pressing. Dad told him that when old timbers bent like that, at some point, the roof would probably fall. Well, part of the roof had already fallen, years before, sealing the mine entrance.

As they approached the center of the chamber, the boys came to a halt and stood in silence. A monstrous object stood menacingly in the center of the main chamber.

42
South Chamber Shaft

The boys stood immobilized at the sight of the massive object in the center of the mine chamber.

"What is it?" Anthony was frozen in astonishment, his mouth agape.

"A . . . giant spider?" Richie whispered.

Corey aimed his Davy lamp at the strange thing. "It's a giant fossil of an ancient tree trunk." He would love to take his time to examine the amazing petrified tree, but his curiosity must wait. Another time, maybe. He pointed to the tunnel straight ahead, beyond the ancient relic. "There's the only shaft they worked in this mine," he said, remembering the drawings on the map. He took out the compass and aimed it in the direction of the chamber. "The shaft is heading due south." His spirits rose. "This is South

Chamber, which should bring us close to the North Star working, where Dad is trapped."

"Let me go first to check the air." Richie disappeared into the dark cavity. After a few minutes he called out, "All clear."

Corey and Anthony followed him, their lights like fireflies flickering in the intense darkness.

The boys walked cautiously, turning their heads to aim the lights from their caps. They searched the walls on each side, hoping to find a fissure or a place where the rock looked different—perhaps with a vein of coal.

"Can't see anything here," Richie said, "just solid rock on each side."

"I know Dad is on the other side of this wall," Corey insisted.

"See if there's a place where there's been some mining," Richie suggested.

"There just has to be something here," Corey said, and he went to the most southerly wall. There was evidence of blasting and picking, but the work had stopped before the wall had been excavated completely.

They came to a section where miners had chopped away several feet into the wall face. He could see a large vein of coal in the rock. "That looks like a vein of anthracite," Corey said, pointing. "I wonder why the mine was abandoned."

"We may never know," Richie answered.

"Maybe Dad is close by." Corey took the pick and banged the wall over and over. He waited for some response—any sound at all—from the other side that might indicate his father was in there.

Nothing.

Anthony banged again, hard and loud, with the spade.

Nothing.

Then Corey remembered talking to his dad about the new international signal for ships. What was it? Save our ship. SOS. Maybe Dad would remember. SOS. They had talked about how they would use it if anyone ever needed help—never thinking that time would come.

Three dots, three dashes, three dots. SOS. Corey took his pick and tapped it on the wall—good and loud, and distinct.

BANG! BANG! BANG! Quickly.

BOOM! BOOM! BOOM! Slowly.

BANG! BANG! BANG! Quickly again.

He tried again.

BANG! BANG! BANG! Quickly.

BOOM! BOOM! BOOM! Slowly.

BANG! BANG! BANG! Quickly again.

Then Corey and his friends waited, listening. Nothing.

Anthony sighed. "There isn't any response, Corey. Should we leave now? I don't see any other fissures or holes other than the one we found."

"Not yet." Corey did not want to leave. "Let's wait a few more minutes." He grabbed the spade and was about to strike the wall again, when he heard something. Dripping water? *Tap, tap, tap*—very faint. "Did you hear that?"

"No, I didn't hear anything," said Richie.

"Me neither," Anthony answered.

"Shh! Don't speak. I heard tapping," Corey insisted.

The boys were silent. The tapping had stopped. After a moment, Corey once again struck the wall.

SOS.

He waited, then did it again.

SOS.

They listened silently for a long minute.

Then, when nothing happened, Richie said, "You know, Corey, I think—"

"Shh!" Corey whispered.

TAP, TAP, TAP, came an answer. Very faint but quick.

POW! POW! POW! came slower sounds.

TAP, TAP, TAP. Three quicker sounds, now more distinct than before.

"Did you hear that?" Corey asked excitedly. "It's Dad. He's heard my signal. He knows it's me. We talked about that new international signal just a few months ago, and we tried it out with my little brothers. It's got to be Dad." Corey's voice trembled. "I know it is."

Corey took the shovel and did the bangs again. Louder this time.

They waited.

Finally, just when Anthony and Richie were about to give up, the tapping started again.

SOS. SOS. SOS.

"See? Dad is answering me!"

43

A Voice from Within the Mountain

Inside the old mine, South Chamber, the three boys listened again for the sound of life beyond the wall of stone.

"I know my father is in there and alive," Corey insisted.

Richie nodded. "What do we do now? How can we get to him?"

Corey began cutting with his pick at the crevice in the wall, where early miners had already swung their picks and axes. The crevice was more than two feet into the face of the wall, and Corey directed his blows into that spot. Repeatedly he chipped away until he thought his arms would break.

"Keep at it, Corey," Anthony said. "I'll shovel away the pieces of stone that fall."

Richie shook his head. "It will take us too long to

open up the rock wall this way. We need manpower and more tools."

"You're right," Corey agreed as he stopped chopping and leaned on the pick.

"I think Richie should go get help," Anthony said.

"Yes, you've got the mule, Richie. Ride back to the colliery. Tell them what we've done and how close we are to reaching my dad."

"Don't let them talk you out of it," Anthony said. "They don't listen to kids like us. Outtalk them!"

"Let them know we're in contact with my father—and to bring men and tools . . . augers and drills—enough to cut through this wall quickly."

Richie nodded, the light from his cap making up-and-down waves on the walls. "I'll go. You keep working. But remember, if the flames on your helmets change color or burst up—or if they go out—then get out of here fast." He headed toward the old gangway.

Corey and Anthony grabbed the picks and chopped at the wall again.

Now and again, Corey banged the shovel with the SOS signal, hoping his dad would know there was help on the way. When there was no return sound from the other side, Corey felt his heart would break. *Hang on, Dad. Hang on.*

Then a few taps showed Corey that, yes, his dad was still alive.

The boys worked in tandem, diligently swinging the picks and clearing away debris, as they waited for the miners to arrive. It was a long wait, and Corey's despair mounted. He felt the mountain over him, with tons of rocks about ready to fall and the smothering sensation that made him gasp for breath. Beads of perspiration broke out on his forehead and slipped down his body like melting ice, while his sweaty hands could no longer get a grip on the pickaxe. Nausea overpowered his thoughts. He threw the pick on the floor and wiped his forehead and hands on his shirt.

"Are you all right, Corey?" Anthony asked.

"Yeah, I'm all right." But he wanted to give in to the panic—to just sink down into the dirt and let go.

He recalled Mrs. Chudzik's words. "I am safe. Nothing is happening to hurt me. Believe it, Corey. Believe in yourself."

He couldn't give up. Corey grabbed the pick from the ground and swung it with a crash against the wall. "I wish they'd hurry."

Anthony stopped working and wiped his sweaty forehead. "Want to stop for a while?"

"No, we can't stop working. Dad is counting on us. So are my mom and my brothers."

Corey gave a huge, angry whack into the fissure with his pick. This time the sound of the pickaxe against the rocks was different. It was hollow, and *echoed* . . . something that did not happen inside a mine.

Anthony noticed too. "That sounded funny."

Corey aimed the light on his cap toward the cavity. "I think we may have broken through."

Anthony looked closely into the hole. "Corey, it seems like you did break through. Just a small hole, but . . . I can't see rock on the other side. I mean . . . it's a hole." He stepped aside so Corey could take a look.

Corey could see only darkness. Could they have broken into the North Star chute? He put his mouth up to the hole and called out, "Dad, are you there? It's me, Corey."

Silence.

Then a voice—weak, not more than a whisper. "Corey, I'm here, son."

44

The Old Mine Comes to Life

Corey and Anthony finally heard voices, tromping footsteps, and the clanking sounds of tools as the old mine came to life.

"We're here, Corey!" It was a familiar voice—Mr. Farley, the fire boss, called in a booming voice.

Corey and Anthony came out from the South Chamber, where they had broken through to the North Star working. A crew arrived and gathered at the central chamber, near the tree fossil. They'd brought a folding canvas stretcher, which they were opening up.

"What took you so long?" Corey asked.

"Oh, I'm sure it seemed like hours to you kids," Mr. Farley answered. "We made it here quickly. Most of us got a ride on Mrs. Chudzik's car. It was something to see—with miners and breaker boys hanging on the bumpers and the trunk. She had at least six or seven of us dangling on, plus three to a seat."

"Mrs. Chudzik's car?" Corey asked.

"Yep. Richie was about to ride on his mule to get help. But Mrs. Chudzik saw him and asked what was happening. Then she offered to take him."

"She left my mother alone?"

"I don't know about your mother. All I know is she offered to take Richie, to get the workers here faster than he could on the mule."

"And what did you say about the breaker boys?"

"They all wanted to come, but we could only take so many on Mrs. Chudzik's car. They want to help you, Corey."

The breaker boys wanted to help him? Corey was stunned.

Before he could ask more, Mr. Farley continued, "Especially those tough kids, Charlie and Frank . . . and the other one. Paddy, that's it. They wouldn't take no for an answer. They think a lot of you, Corey."

"Show us where you broke through to the North Star—where you think you heard your dad," a miner said.

Corey took the men into the South Chamber and showed them the hole in the wall. "He's in there, but I haven't heard from him since." Corey put his mouth to the hole and called out, "Dad, there's a crew here now to get you out. They're coming, Dad!"

There was no answer.

From the way the miners looked at one another, it

seemed they didn't believe that his father had answered him earlier, or they feared Dad hadn't survived. "He answered me just before you came," Corey insisted. "Please, get him out."

Mr. Farley cleared his throat and hollered. "You heard the boy. Get to work and break through this wall." He turned to Corey again. "We won't blast with dynamite. It could bring this old roof down on top of everyone. So we're going to dig—just like you did, Corey, but we have drills and augers to make the work faster."

Corey didn't want to leave the chamber. He wanted to be around when they found his father. Then another thought occurred to him. He turned to Mr. Farley and asked, "How will we get Dad out of the mine? The only way we know is up through the pipe."

"It would be hard to pull a stretcher carrying Joe up through that pipe, especially if he has injuries," Mr. Farley agreed. "Richie told us to bring strong but skinny men, to get down that pipe. Take a look around the mine, Corey. When the Avondale mine caught on fire in 1899, there was only one exit, and that was blocked by fire. One hundred ten men died." He shook his head. "We learned a lot from that disaster because afterward a law was enacted that mines must have at least two exits. This law wasn't in effect when they started mining here, but common sense might have ruled. If so, there might be another outlet. Why don't you go look?"

"We did most of the work already," Anthony whispered

as they headed out into the main chamber with their tools. "They always want to get rid of us kids."

They searched the walls of the gangway and around the tree fossil for signs of another tunnel but could find nothing. Then Corey had an idea. "Wait a minute. There were circles on the map—one where the pipe is located, and another off to the other side. When we came down the pipe to the passageway, we turned to the right at the bottom. But the path also went off to the left, where the other circle is shown on the map."

"That's right," Richie said. "We don't know what's on the other side of that pipe."

"Let's go see where that other end of the path will take us," Corey said. "Those circles on the map might show air vents. If so, there should be one at the end of the path beyond the pipe."

As the boys headed into the passageway and retraced their steps to the pipe, Corey asked Richie, "Were you able to get out of the pipe easily?"

"Let me tell you that Abby is as strong as an angry heifer. She pulled me up so fast I thought I'd end up on the moon." They reached the pipe, and Richie pointed ahead. "See? This passage continues."

"Let's follow it. Maybe we'll find another way out," Corey said, moving on.

The three friends continued walking. Richie led the way with his Davy light piercing the blackness. The path was gradually leading uphill.

Where was this pathway taking them? Would it just

lead to a dead end? *No, this passage was not carved or blasted out of sheer rock just to go nowhere,* Corey told himself. There had to be a reason. There must be an exit or something ahead.

Richie stopped suddenly. "We're at the end of the path. There's only a wall in front of me."

"Is it stone?" Corey asked, disappointed.

Richie gave the wall a blow with his pick. "No. It's soft—like soil or dirt or maybe moss."

"Shh! Listen," Anthony whispered. "I hear something."

The boys were silent.

Then Richie said, "I hear a howling sound—like the wind."

Anthony disagreed. "No, it's an animal, and we're heading right into its den."

"It's more like someone knocking," Corey insisted.

For a moment, the boys were silent again. Then they exclaimed in unison, "The knockers!"

45
Babcia

The boys trembled in the narrow passageway. "There's no such thing as knockers," Corey said after a few moments. "Mrs. Chudzik said so. And she knows everything."

"So what is it, then?" Anthony asked.

"It doesn't matter," Corey said. "We need to find another exit, and this might be the way. It's not hard stone here. Move aside, Richie. Let me see." He took his own pick and poked at the wall in front of them. Dirt and moss fell out onto the floor.

"It's the end of the tunnel," Anthony said.

"If we pick away at this, it may be an opening," Corey said. Then he had a horrible thought. "What if it's the river behind this wall? If we let in the river, it would flood the mine and drown everyone."

"Are we near the river?" Anthony asked.

"We're heading in that direction," said Corey.

"Then what should we do?" Richie said.

Corey recalled the circles on the map that Mr. Russell had made. One was obviously the pipe they had used to enter the mine. "There were two circles—one is where the pipe is, which they think was for ventilation, and one was this place at the end of the path. So if the circles show ventilation, then the one here, at the end of the path, must be a way to get air into the mine too—maybe to keep this whole area clear of gases."

"Do we dare take the chance?" Richie asked.

Corey reached out with his hand and felt the wall ahead of them. It was mossy and damp.

"The wailing and knocking we heard might come from an animal den. If it is, then it's not the river," Anthony suggested.

"I'll chop away some more." Corey was already hacking at the barrier. "I'll do fifty chops, and then we'll see if there are any signs of water." One, two, three . . . the dirt poured out in clumps and roots and soil and collected on the floor of the tunnel.

"If you do fifty chops, the whole thing could cave in on us, and then what?" Anthony asked. "The river would blow us off our feet and we'd drown."

"Don't even think about it," Corey said, remembering how the thought of the river filling the mine had sent him into a panic.

"We have the walls around us," Richie said. "The dirt can't fill up this whole tunnel, can it?"

Corey continued picking away at the dirt wall in front of him. "We can always run back, if it becomes a landslide."

"But not if it's the river," Anthony moaned.

"Oh, now I've lost count. I'll just keep at it until I get tired," Corey said. The dirt was piling up, and he stepped back. "Let's get this out of the way somehow."

Richie turned his pick sideways and pulled the dirt away with it. "I should have brought a shovel."

Corey chopped feverishly. "Just make do. I've got to find if this goes anywhere."

"Or you may be opening into a den of wolves or bears," Anthony muttered.

Corey stopped to listen. "I hear those scratching and moaning sounds again."

"They're louder and closer, too," Richie agreed.

Corey punched the dirt in front of him, and more dirt and clay flowed out. "I can see roots," he said. "We're under a tree or something with roots."

"It's been years since anyone dug anything around here," Anthony noted. "Trees have taken root and grown. At least it's not the river."

"Now I wish we had a saw and an axe." Corey stopped to wipe the sweat off his forehead. "Maybe one of you can go back and get them. We're so close, and all we have is picks. It will take forever to cut away tree roots with picks."

"I'll go," Anthony said. "I'll see if someone brought a rake, too."

"You can't carry all that by yourself. Why don't both of you go—and you can find out if they've broken through that South Chamber wall and found my dad."

"Will you be all right?" Anthony asked.

"Sure, I'm all right. I'm going to get Dad out of this place. I just hope . . . it's not too late." Corey's voice broke and he swallowed hard. "Go on. Both of you. Get the tools and tell the others what we've found here. Hurry."

"We'll be back soon," Anthony promised.

"I'll keep pounding away until you get back." Corey could already hear the fading sounds of their footsteps as he wielded his pick at the dirt wall ahead of him.

Corey had no idea how much time passed as he whacked away at the soil. It was almost up to his knees where it had fallen into the passageway. He came upon a root that was knotted around itself, and this time he angrily concentrated on it. After picking at it, he let the tine of the pickaxe hook onto the root and held on, pulling and yanking at the root with all the strength he had left. Suddenly it gave way, crashing to the ground. Corey stood in the muddy passageway and stared out into the hole it had created. It *was* a tree. The lower branches had filled the passage.

He reached out into the gap where the piles of dirt had been and pulled away the fallen foliage, and looked up. He could see the sky. "I found the way out."

He pulled himself into the gaping hole and wiggled through the dirt and vegetation and found himself looking down the steep hill to the river. It was getting dark and lights were coming on along the shore.

Corey wanted to dance with excitement. There was now a way to get his father out of the mine.

Then, to his astonishment, he heard a whine and a bark.

Hovi!

The dog jumped over the tree and vegetation to Corey. Whimpering all the while, Hovi lapped Corey's face and pawed his leg. Corey hugged the dog, who barked and cried in delight, while his tail made circles.

"So it was you who made those sounds. But how did you know I was under the ground here? How did you know that was me inside there, trying to get out?" Corey laughed and cried as the dog whined happily.

"Corey! You found the way out!"

Corey looked up to see Mrs. Chudzik standing nearby. She was there for him as she always was.

Corey's eyes filled with tears. Perhaps he had called her the name in his dreams—or perhaps it was stamped on his brain, or it was just meant to be—but it wasn't a bit strange or awkward. It felt comfortable and right as he cried out the Polish word for "grandma" and ran into her arms. "Babcia!"

46
Waiting

How did Hovi find me?" Corey asked Babcia later as he hugged and petted the dog.

"I have no idea. But he knew somehow. He's been looking for another way to get to you. He stayed close to that tunnel that you just came from for hours, pawing and whining. He knew that was a way to get to you."

"Good boy, Hovi," Corey said. "My good dog."

"Did they find your father?" Babcia asked.

"They're opening up the wall between the two mines. It shouldn't take much longer. Does Mom know about any of this?"

"She knows, but she's a miner's wife and daughter. She's doing her best to stay calm. Come to my house when you can. She needs to know you are both safe."

At that moment, Corey heard someone calling, "Corey! Corey! Where are you?" It was Anthony.

"I'm here!" Corey ran to the side of the cliff, where Anthony stood looking around. "Any news about Dad?"

"Good news, Corey," Anthony said. "They got him out of the North Star shaft, and he's down near the fossil tree." He grabbed Corey. "Just a few injuries and some burns. He's goin' to be all right."

"Do they know about this exit?"

"They do now. Richie and I came looking for you. When we saw you found the way out, Richie went back to tell the others. Mr. Farley said to tell you to wait outside, and they'll bring your dad very soon. They're bandaging him up."

It was almost dark when Richie joined them. The air was fresh and a new moon was rising. The world was peaceful with the scent of hemlocks.

A dozen or so people were outside waiting to see if there would be a rescue, including Abby and her father. Mr. Russell disappeared off and on into the mine through the new opening.

There were no crowds like there were in the big disasters. This was only one man caught in a roof fall. "This won't make the headlines," someone said, "but it does have a good share of heroes."

Richie suddenly appeared in the gaping hole Corey had created. "Pretty soon, Corey," he said with a grin. "Everything looks good!" He stretched, then said, "I'm worried about Tootsie. I'm gonna take her down for some water and let her know I haven't forgotten her."

"Tootsie helped pull you up from the mine," Abby reminded him. "I tied the rope on her harness, and she knew she had to pull."

"That's how I got up so fast!" Richie said, kissing Tootsie on the nose. He climbed on her back and headed down the footpath, singing, "Toot, toot, Tootsie, good-bye."

A dark-haired woman rushed up the hill. When she caught sight of Anthony, she screamed, "Anthony! Thanks be to God. You are alive!" She began speaking in Italian as she ran to Anthony, kissing him, mussing his hair, and crying all the while.

Anthony talked softly, trying to comfort her. "I'm fine, Mama. Corey, Richie, and I are all fine. We've just been busy helping Corey to rescue his papa."

"Is he alive?" Anthony's mama asked, tears streaming down her cheeks.

"He's gonna be fine—*bono*—*bello*," Anthony assured her.

Babcia stepped closer and put her arm on the woman's shoulder. "Your boy helped save Corey's father."

Anthony's mother looked up, and when she saw Mrs. Chudzik, she moved away. "Don't touch me!"

"Mrs. Chudzik has been here all day, Mama," Anthony explained hastily. "She helped us save Mr. Adamski."

"You come on home now," Anthony's mother ordered, grabbing him by the ear. "Your papa's waitin' for you." She shoved him ahead of her as he stumbled down the hill toward home.

Corey knew Dad would tell Anthony's father what a good friend Anthony had been, and how he had stayed by Corey's side throughout the whole long ordeal.

Corey found a boulder near the newly discovered mine entrance and sat. He thought about Richie and how he and Tootsie had helped save Dad. And how Abby had stood by faithfully until it was all over. He looked around, but Abby was gone.

Nothing I can ever say or do would be adequate to thank my friends—all of them—including those tough breaker boys who were so eager to help.

Corey found his eyes slipping closed. He did not feel sleepy, but his whole body ached and sleep wanted to take over.

The moon was high overhead when he finally heard cheers.

"Your dad is up from the mine," someone whispered to him. "He's asking for you, Corey."

From the opening that Corey discovered, Charlie and his pals emerged, carrying his father out of the mine. They set the stretcher on the ground.

"This here's your dad, kid," Charlie said, his voice quavering.

Corey, stumbling over the rough terrain, ran to his father and knelt by him.

"I heard how you found me, Corey," his father whispered. "You figured it all out; you didn't give up, and you tracked me down. What a great butty you are, Corey." A smile flickered over his face.

Corey put his face against his father's cheek. He tried to speak, but he shook so badly the words could not come out.

"It's all right, Corey," Dad whispered. "Everything is all right now."

47
Something Missing

The next few days, Corey and Dad stayed in the Chudzik mansion. Jack and Sammy were at home with Aunt Millie, who came to stay so the boys could still go to school. Things were hazy in Corey's mind, since he slept for the better part of two days. He had no nightmares, but he heard faint voices, Hovi's barks, and a baby's cries.

When he finally awoke, he was in soft, clean pajamas— not the nightshirt Mom had made from discarded muslin from the mine. How did that happen?

Barefoot, he hurried down the winding stairway. Soft laughter drifted from the parlor, and seeing the open door, Corey peered in. The draperies, pulled back from the open window, let in the sweet scent of spring earth. A bright cheerfulness filled the room. But something was different. What was it?

Mom was nestled in a big rocking chair and holding a pink bundle. "Come here, Corey," Mom said, one arm out-stretched.

He moved quickly across the thick Persian rug and let his mother hug him. She planted a kiss on his cheek and then held the baby out for him to see. "You have a little sister. Isn't she beautiful?"

Corey touched the tiny hands with their perfect pink-and-white nails. The baby stretched, scrunched up her face and eyes, and went back to sleep while sunbeams danced on her golden hair.

"Sit down, Corey," Mrs. Chudzik said, pulling up an armchair. "I'm sure you and your mother have much to talk about." She left the parlor and closed the door quietly.

"Put your arms out and hold our little girl." She handed the baby over to Corey. "Support her head," she instructed as she adjusted the baby's blanket. Corey sat stiffly in the chair, afraid to move for fear of dropping the baby, but soon he relaxed. "Does she have a name yet?"

"Not quite," Mom answered. "Perhaps there's a name you like."

Corey thought about the girls' names from school. *Mary, Helen, Margaret, Ruth, Frances, and Bertha. They're ordinary names. My sister is no ordinary baby. She should have a beautiful name.*

Mom interrupted his thoughts. "There's a Polish name

that Dad thinks is perfect for our baby. Babcia says it means 'blonde.'"

"What is it?" Corey asked.

"Albinka," Mom answered, a grin playing on her lips. "Dad said we'd call her Binky for short."

Corey's mouth dropped open. "Mom, please don't give her that name." Corey looked closely at the baby. No way did he want his beautiful little sister stuck with that name. Corey tried to be tactful, considering it was Dad's choice, as he struggled for the right words. "Um . . . she doesn't look like Albinka, and she's definitely not a Binky."

Mom nodded. "That makes three of us who do not want Albinka."

Later, Mrs. Chudzik brought in sandwiches and tea on her squeaky tea cart, then left.

Mom put the baby in the cradle and rocked her for a few minutes.

Corey suddenly realized what was different about the parlor. How could he have missed it? The coffin was gone! "Mom, did you get to see the coffin? Where did it go?"

"The parlor was always closed while I was here, so I never laid eyes on it," Mom said. "But early the other morning I heard a truck outside and a commotion from this room. After that, the parlor door was open, with the sweet little cradle placed right there in the middle of the room. There was not a sign of the coffin."

"Did she tell you why she had the coffin in here in the first place?" Corey asked.

"No, she never said a word about the coffin, but she did tell me some things."

"What?"

"She said you told her that we all loved her." They were both silent for a while. Then Mom said, "Maybe Babcia doesn't need the coffin anymore now that she has us for a family." She looked off, remembering. "She said something else."

"What was that?"

"She said that although she saved *your* life, *you* saved *her* life too."

48
Hope

Later, when the family was back home together, Corey noticed how cautious and nervous Dad was about holding the baby. "She's not made of glass, Dad."

"She's so little—and fragile," Dad said.

"Dad, are you happy with a little girl? Instead of another boy, I mean?"

"Of course I'm happy. We always wanted a little girl."

"I know how to play with my brothers," Corey said, "but I don't know much about girls."

"There are different concerns with little girls than there are with boys. Boys need to grow up and be strong and tough. But girls are delicate and sensitive, and it's our duty as men to protect our girls."

Corey thought of Abby and how pretty and sweet she

was and how the boys picked on her. But hadn't she hit Billy with her purse and sent him home crying with a nosebleed? And how many boys would be braver than she had been when she'd fallen into the shaft on the hill and pulled herself out?

Girls can take care of themselves very well, he decided with a grin.

The baby's name was the subject of a family meeting. Aunt Millie and Babcia were included in the discussion.

"I thought we named her Albinka," Dad said, as if it were all settled. "Binky for short."

"Albinka?" Aunt Millie said. "We've never had an Albinka in the family."

Aunt Millie is hoping the baby will be named for her, Corey thought.

"You chose Albinka and never once asked what my choice might be," Mom said, standing up. "I am the one who gave birth to this baby girl, so I have earned the right to my opinion. We need a meaningful name—"

"Meaningful?" Dad interrupted. "She's a girl. Shouldn't she have a cute name like Binky?"

"Yeah, we like Binky!" Jack yelled.

"We want Binky," Sammy agreed. "Binky! Binky!"

Mom ignored the interruption. "This has been a difficult year for our family. Corey had to quit school to work at the breaker; he nearly drowned and suffered with terrors we can't even imagine. Then there was the cave-in and the anxiety that went with it—not knowing if Dad was dead or alive.

"But one thing that kept our family strong was hope. Hope is like an anchor that holds us firm during life's storms. I would like our baby's first name to be Hope."

There was silence as the family thought about Mom's words.

But Mom wasn't finished. Before anyone could speak, she continued, "We have been blessed with a loving new grandma who saved Corey's life and is helping him overcome his phobia. She believed in him so that he believed in himself—which in turn gave him the strength to go into the uncharted mine to find his father."

Mom gestured to Mrs. Chudzik. "And then our babcia safely brought our baby into the world. They are both God's gift to us. I'd like to name Hope after Babcia as well. Her full name will be Hope Alexandra Adamski."

Mom and the boys cheered. Babcia's eyes shone. Aunt Millie didn't appear too happy, but she shrugged and nodded.

Then Dad stood up and made the announcement. "Hope Alexandra Adamski is our daughter's name."

Hovi, who was sleeping at Corey's feet, thumped his tail in agreement.

49
Happy House

Lots of great things happened that spring.

Because Dad had such an impressive knowledge of the old mines in the area, he was offered a job as assistant to Mr. Russell. Then, with a better salary, he could spend more time with his family. Corey went back to school.

Babcia and Mom were best friends, and like best friends, they needed to be in close contact every day. So Babcia had phones installed in both houses. "In case of emergency," she said. But Corey noticed that Mom checked with Babcia at least three times every day to discuss . . . whatever it was that best friends talk about.

This morning, Babcia rang Mom to tell her good news. The new hospital committee had asked her to be president and coordinator. They felt Babcia would be an asset to the town because of her medical background and her tireless assistance during the recent cave-in.

"People wave to Babcia when she drives around town," Corey noticed. "They don't run and hide anymore."

Hovi was a hero once word got out that he'd found the other exit in the old mine before anyone. A picture of him, sitting by the newly discovered mine opening, was in newspapers all over the state. Everyone in Pennsylvania knew all about Hovi, and the word "hellhound" was no longer in the local vocabulary.

The old gray mansion with the turrets took on a new look. Babcia had her house painted a pretty shade of rosy tan—the front door was a sunny yellow. Corey, as he had promised, planted bright flowers and shrubs around the building. On the front porch, a large welcome mat now greeted the world.

Once Corey no longer worked at the mine, his phobia slowly faded away. He wondered if someday it might return, but in the meantime, it had lost most of its power over him.

The breaker boys' team won the valley championship, thanks to the Slavic boys, who knocked the ball out of the park several times. Corey did his share with a few good hits, and the team celebrated their victory in the big yard at Mrs. Chudzik's no-longer-spooky mansion.

Nothing in the old house was strange or dark anymore, including the ugly knocker on the front door. It was polished to a shiny finish and had stopped scowling at visitors.

"This old knocker is smiling," Abby whispered one

day—as if the knocker could hear her. "It actually looks quite cheerful." She looked at Corey with questioning eyes. "Dad says we heard echoes of miners striking at the walls of the Mountain Crest mine because the two mines were so close. What do you think, Corey? Did we really hear the knockers? Or were they just echoes?"

"Abby, *everyone* knows there are no echoes in the mines," Corey reminded her.

Hovi, who was at Corey's side, barked and wagged his tail.

"Hovi believes in the knockers," Abby said.

Corey patted the dog's head. "Hovi has been in on all the secrets around here, right from the start."

"So you and I and Hovi know the knockers exist, but no one will *ever* believe us," Abby said with a sigh.

"*We* know, and that's all that matters, anyway." Corey pulled up the handle on the brass knocker. "Shall we?"

Abby nodded and Corey let it go.

KNOCK! KNOCK! KNOCK!

❖

Afterword

Several years ago I lived in a small town near Boston. One day I was told by someone who knew the history of the town that a woman doctor lived there back in the 1800s and was known as "the casket lady." She was famous for having a massive, carved casket in her parlor. Although I didn't pay much attention to the story, I must have tucked it away in my memory, because it popped into my brain as I began writing *Breaker Boy*.

Recently I told the tale to friends who live in the town. They looked into the town archives and sent me information that verified the story I had heard so long ago. The woman was a doctor who did keep a coffin in her parlor. The casket was described as being of Gothic design and so creepy with its carved creatures that it was perfect for my book!

I gave a Polish surname, Chudzik, to the Coffin Lady in my book because my story takes place in the anthracite coal region of Northeastern Pennsylvania, where miners and their families of Polish, Welsh, and other nationalities labored and lived.

You may already know how bituminous and anthracite coal were formed. Over the centuries, as ancient forest vegetation died and dropped into the soil, layers of earth covered it, and after many years the pressure of the heavy layers turned the soil into peat moss, soft (bituminous) coal, or hard (anthracite) coal, where the imprints of the ancient foliage can sometimes be seen. Ancient inhabitants discovered the moss and coal made good fuel, so they used it for cooking, heating, and for manufacturing pottery and weapons.

During the Industrial Revolution, when the power of steam and electricity was discovered, there was still a need for coal. Bituminous was the most used because of its availability and lower cost. However, it was dirty, and the air in cities like London was unhealthy. The thick dust covered everything, and people became sick.

Anthracite coal was not as obtainable as bituminous and was more expensive. However, it was preferred because it was hard and burned hotter and cleaner. There were many bituminous mines in the world, but anthracite could be found in fewer areas. In the United States, for example, it is only found in Northeastern Pennsylvania.

Hardworking miners risked their lives to dig out the "black diamonds." Dangerous working conditions, roof falls, flooding, and explosions often took their lives. Coal left its sickening marks in the lungs of mine workers with deadly "black lung disease."

Mine workers were not paid adequately for the dangers they faced. They worked long hours, digging out tons of coal by hand, until late in the nineteenth century, when the bituminous coal miners formed a union: the United Mine Workers of America. In 1902 members of the union who worked in the anthracite coalfields went on strike. This was known as the Anthracite Coal Strike.

This strike caused vicious fights between the union members and the nonstrikers. The hatred between various ethnic groups became deadly. The "coal barons," or the owners of the mines, were against the strikers. Some miners were killed and others were hung. It was a dark, deadly, and dangerous period of time.

The National Guard, local police, and detective agencies became involved in the war that was being fought in Pennsylvania. Things became so bad that President Theodore Roosevelt had to intervene. The miners finally prevailed, receiving a 10 percent wage increase and a reduced workday, from ten to nine hours per day.

Today there is another method of mining called "strip mining," which mines the coal seams that are close to the surface instead of blasting into the mountain itself. This type of mining leaves huge craters and an ugly landscape as well as causing other environmental issues. The law requires that when mining is finished in these fields, the mine area must be filled and restored to its original condition.

You can find interesting information about anthracite mining by visiting the Anthracite Heritage Museum in Scranton, Pennsylvania. Or you can visit it online at anthracitemuseum.org. The Anthracite Heritage Museum serves educational needs regarding the story of hard coal mining, its related industries, and the immigrant culture of Northeastern Pennsylvania.

You may also want to visit the Eckley Miners' Village Museum in Weatherly, Pennsylvania, which was founded in 1854. Here you can see an actual town with its patch village and company store: eckleyminersvillage.com.

Mining communities often had a company store that was owned by the mining companies. The mine workers were paid with "scrip"—money that had the inscription of the mine. The workers could only purchase their groceries and goods from the company store. It was not legal tender, so other community stores would not accept the phony money. The miners were trapped into purchasing from their employer's store, where the prices and the interest were high. Often the purchases exceeded a miner's pay, so the family would go without until the next payday.

There have been many folk tales and songs about the company store. The chorus of one popular song, "Sixteen Tons," was made a hit by Tennessee Ernie Ford back in the 1950s.

"You load sixteen tons, what do you get?
Another day older and deeper in debt.
Saint Peter don't you call me 'cause I can't go.
I owe my soul to the company store."

Because "Sixteen Tons" told the history of American mining and became so well known, it is considered an American folk song.

Corey's drowning experience left him with a condition known today as Post Traumatic Stress Disorder, or PTSD. We often hear of veterans who suffer this condition after serving in war zones. Back in the days of World War I, an abnormal fear that recalled the horrors of war was called "shell shock."

Fear is a normal emotion and is a way to protect oneself when facing a dangerous situation. But when a person has PTSD, an abnormal fear still lingers in the brain, taking over and making a person frightened even when there is no danger or very little danger. Usually the panic associated with the fear is brought on by hidden memories that are awakened, and the patient feels as if the terrifying incidents are happening again.

Phobias have been around since ancient times. Hippocrates, who lived around 400 BCE, had a patient who would panic at the sound of a flute. Strangely, hearing the sound of a flute at night didn't bother the man. Where does the word "phobia" come from? The ancient Greeks had a god named Phobos, who was so frightening that soldiers would paint his ugly picture on their shields, hoping to scare away their enemies. A definition of the word "phobia" as we think of it today is "a fear, horror, strong dislike, or aversion; especially an extreme or irrational fear or dread aroused by a particular object or circumstance."

Phobias are sometimes treated the way Mrs. Chudzik helped Corey. Facing up to the fear very gradually, under the care of a physician, helps the patient realize that the fear is unfounded, and can often lessen or even remove the problem. Severe phobias and panic attacks are usually treated by a psychiatrist, who may do brain scans and prescribe medication.

Some of the symptoms of PTSD and phobias are nightmares, flashbacks, upsetting images, distressing thoughts, sweating, rapid heartbeat, and nausea. These symptoms are often triggered by feelings, words, thoughts, or even smells that bring back memories of the original event—just like Corey's fear of being trapped under the ice.

In my fictional story, Corey recovers gradually, as he realizes that the danger isn't always present when he has a panic attack. Once he begins to recognize that the fear is unsupported, it loses much of the power it had over him. However, people with PTSD may need medical help for prolonged periods of time. Yes, a phobia and PTSD can take away the very joy of life. It is a real medical condition.

Did you know there really is a German breed of dog called "Hovawart"? There are records and stories of Hovawarts that trace the breed as far back as the 1200s, relating their bravery and loyalty. The name reflects their qualities; it means "guardian of the estate." Hovawarts were almost wiped out by World War I, but they are being brought back by those who love the breed.

You can see pictures and read about this loyal and hardworking dog on the Internet. Friends of mine own a Hovawart named Django. When I first met Django, he scared me with his deep-throated and rancorous bark. I could easily believe he was the guardian of the estate! Now he greets me with kisses, plus a wagging tail that seems to make a full circle. Django has stolen my heart— and the hearts of our neighbors and friends. I just *had* to have a Hovawart like Django in the book.

The stories of knockers have been around for centuries. They originated in the coal countries of Europe and England hundreds of years ago. The small elves were said to warn of roof falls. Other stories blamed the knockers for accidents, cave-ins, and stolen equipment. Some men who wanted to stay on the right side of the knockers would share their lunches with them, leaving cookies or pieces of cake in the mines at the end of their day.

You may have seen knockers in the Walt Disney movie *Snow White and the Seven Dwarfs*. The seven dwarfs, with their tiny shovels and picks, go off to work in the mine singing, "Heigh-ho, heigh-ho, it's off to work we go." They were not coal miners, however. And I don't remember them knocking. Instead, those little fellows worked in diamond mines, where they would "dig, dig, dig a-dig dig."

Acknowledgments

Thanks, thanks, and more thanks to the Krane (Kraynanski) family from Wilkes-Barre who grew up in the anthracite coal mine country and who related generations of their family's stories of coal mining history. The colorful and multiethnic groups, the plight of miners and their wives, the boys who worked at the breaker, the history-making strikes, and the community itself lured me to use this setting for my book. *Dziękuję!*

Thanks to John and Bertha Osterhaven from Wilmington, Massachusetts, who researched the town archives and confirmed the strange story of the "casket lady" that I heard many years ago.

Thank you, Venice Library children's department, for the fun we had as I tried out the first few chapters of this story on a local Girl Scout troop. This eager audience begged me to finish the book. Since *Breaker Boy* is somewhat different from my other novels, their enthusiasm was especially encouraging.

Special cheers go to my bright, creative editor, Ruta Rimas, for her thoughts and encouragement with the development of the manuscript; and to Natascha Morris, her competent and super-helpful assistant.

As always, my deep appreciation to authors June Fiorelli, Gail Hedrick, and Betty Conard, my loyal writing group from Sarasota, Florida, for kind critique and for cheering me on.

—J. H. H.